It was more than unsettling for Cole to be kissing someone else. A part of her wanted to scream, "Stop!" But the part of her that hurt gave way.

"Don't be nervous, babe," Tray said, kissing her neck.

"I'm not," she lied.

Tray ran her fingers through Cole's hair. "Love your hair. Such beautiful curls and waves." Tray kissed her again. "So pretty," she whispered.

Cole closed her eyes to the kisses. She let feelings of anxious passion carry her into the moment and away from any doubt.

Tray blew out a candle. The shadows fell gray in the dusk, but Cole could still see the eyes that took her in. Tray wrapped Cole in her arms, the kisses more urgent, the grip of fingers into Cole's flesh pulling them closer together until Cole could feel Tray's body warm against her own.

LOOKING FOR NAIAD?

**Buy our books at
www.naiadpress.com**

**or call our toll-free number
1-800-533-1973**

**or by fax (24 hours a day)
1-850-539-9731**

INTIMATE STRANGER

BY
LAURA DEHART YOUNG

THE NAIAD PRESS, INC.
1999

Printed in the United States of America on acid-free paper
First Edition

Editor: Christine Cassidy
Cover designer: Bonnie Liss (Phoenix Graphics)
Typesetter: Sandi Stancil

Library of Congress Cataloging-in-Publication Data

Young, Laura DeHart, 1956 –
   Intimate stranger / Laura DeHart Young.
      p.   cm.
   ISBN 1-56280-249-6   (alk. paper)
   I. Title.
PS3575.O799I58   1999
813'.54—dc21   98-48235
                                                         CIP

For Jerri
Nobody lives without love

About the Author

Laura DeHart Young currently has five romance novels published with Naiad Press: *There Will be No Goodbyes*, *Family Secrets*, *Love on the Line*, *Private Passions* and her newest book, *Intimate Stranger*. Her sixth romance novel, *Forever and the Night*, will be published by Naiad Press in 2000. When not writing for Naiad, Laura works as a communications manager for a worldwide information company. She lives in Atlanta, Georgia with her Pug, Dudley.

Chapter One

The platform of the second-story fire escape was her best angle. Directly below, a large crowd had gathered, pushing toward the four-car wreck in the shape of an ameba. Police and ambulance lights flashed. From the point where a body lay in a fetal position, an irregular pattern of red flowed. Someone finally covered the deceased soul with a light blue tarp. *Click, whir, click, whir.* Through the camera lens Cole Evans saw the twisted metal of what was once a Jeep Cherokee turned in the opposite direction from where it had been traveling. Not far away was a white Ford truck, broadsided and wrapped like a horseshoe around a utility pole. Finally, when she knew she had taken enough photographs, she shimmied alongside the fire escape and quickly lowered herself onto the rusted ladder. About twenty steps down, she dropped to the alleyway below. She jogged through the alley toward the adjoining street. Picking her way through the crowd, she scurried toward the police cars blocking the western end of the intersection.

"Hey, Evans! My mug gonna make the paper again?"

Cole hoisted the faded green backpack over her shoulder. Involuntarily, she smiled. It was Campo, short for Officer Joe Campognolli, assigned to the 15th precinct.

"Campo, looks like you've got your hands full."

He took off his blue cap and scratched his head. "Aw, hell — just another day in downtown Chicago. This gonna be on the front page tomorrow morning?"

"Most likely. The local section."

Car horns beeped. Rush hour traffic was only beginning. People were leaning out their car windows, yelling obscenities.

"Awright, awright already," Campo said, twirling his stout body toward the ruckus. "Man, I better get goin' here. See ya later, sport."

"Till next time, Campo. Take it easy."

"Out here? You gotta be kiddin' me."

Cole chuckled and mocked a stiff salute. "Later."

Heading in the direction of her car, Cole stopped abruptly when she heard another familiar voice. It was Kay Stewart, photographer for the *Sun-Times*. Kay grabbed her by the shoulders and smiled. "Cole, where have you been hiding?"

"On fire escapes."

"Very funny."

Cole gave her a bear hug. "How are you?"

"Great. So good to see you."

Kay was tall and muscular with long, auburn hair. They often ran into each other on the job and after hours at some of the downtown lesbian clubs. They had developed a casual friendship that was easy and fun. "You're as beautiful as ever."

Kay frowned and said, "Yeah, but you don't visit me anymore. After all, the *Trib* and the *Sun-Times* are right across the street from each other. So what's your excuse?"

"Afraid someone will see me and think I'm switching allegiances."

"That's pretty lame."

"Maybe we could meet halfway."

Kay squeezed Cole's hand. "Anytime you'd like. We can meet on the corner of Michigan Avenue and try to beat the raising bridge."

"Sounds like an adventure worth having."

"With you, it would be. Hey, I gotta run. But you keep in touch, hear?"

In her car, Cole executed a quick U-turn in the middle of the street, trying to avoid patches of ice and snow. She headed in the opposite direction, knowing full well what was happening the other way. The '93 Honda Civic handled well as she cut from one lane to another, detoured down side streets and alleys, dodging the five o'clock rush. She dug around the passenger seat next to her and grabbed her cell phone. A half-minute later, one of the *Chicago Tribune*'s central operators put her through to the photo lab.

"Marty, it's Cole. Hey, I'm heading home now to develop the film of this accident. I'll have the prints to you by eleven."

"Yeah, good. Sheila will want 'em scanned by then. And you know Barnes. He don't like to wait neither." Marty wheezed and hissed air into the phone. Chronic asthma.

"Hey, no problem."

"You know how those two get," he said. Wheeze, cough. "Everything's gotta be copacetic by two A.M. for the first edition. Sheila sent out another memo today."

"Oh, gosh. Well, don't sweat it. Haven't missed one of Sheila's deadlines yet. See you in a few."

"Yeah, okay. Get some good stuff?"

"Listen, it's been quite a day. And if you call a dead body in the subway this morning and a tangled mess of cars and blood in the streets this afternoon 'good stuff,' yes — I got some great stuff."

Cole pulled her car into the driveway that ran perpendicular to the house. Jan was home. Her red Miata still looked brand new, gleaming in the last sunlight of the day. Grabbing her camera bag, backpack, newspaper and gloves, Cole trudged toward the back of the house, the snow crunching beneath her boots. She juggled the keys in her hands and dropped them twice before finally opening the door.

She smelled food, onions and spices. Her stomach growled accordingly as she dragged herself through the entranceway. Everything that was once attached to her shoulder slipped onto the floor beside her.

"Cole, please don't dump your stuff inside the door. I'm tired of tripping over it."

The stern, though always sultry, voice came from the kitchen. "Okay, okay. What kind of greeting is that?"

Suddenly, Jan was standing in the kitchen doorway. Her dark hair bounced over her shoulders, and she leaned her hip against the doorjamb. "Sorry. How was your day?"

"Busy. A little crazy, actually. And yours?"

Jan's five-foot-five frame was dressed in an expensive Jones of New York navy suit. The suit darkened her eyes, normally a cobalt blue. That was the first memory Cole had of Jan — those blue eyes, as clear as an October sky, staring into hers from across a crowded room. Jan could mesmerize a room full of people just by making an entrance. All heads would move in unison, following her confident stride. Jan kissed her lightly on the forehead. "My day was the same. Picked up some Chinese food on the way home. That okay?"

"Perfect. Thanks." Cole leaned against the kitchen counter as Jan unpacked the food. She stared at the freckled complexion, perfectly chiseled nose and full lips. "I miss —" Cole stopped. She had been thinking how much she missed Jan's touch. The words had spilled out before she could catch herself.

Jan gazed at her sideways. She kissed Cole lightly on the cheek and handed her two dinner plates. "Miss what?"

With a shrug, Cole accepted the dinner plates. "The warm weather. It's gotten so cold. Happened

5

overnight. One day it's August, next thing you know it's the end of January."

Jan laughed, a throaty laugh that made Cole smile. "Cole, you belong on an island somewhere. Chicago is definitely not the city for you."

"Oh, you know I love Chicago. Even the cold weather — once I get used to it." Cole shook her head. "That's me. Can't ever seem to make up my mind."

They sat in the small dining area just off the kitchen. Candlelight reflected in those electric blue eyes as Jan recounted her day with a new client. She worked for an interior design firm downtown and had just purchased her own percentage of the business.

"Difficult. That's the only word that comes to mind." Jan sipped her spring water. "But then, that describes half my clientele, I suppose." Peppering her fried rice, Jan's tone became increasingly animated. "I suggested knocking out the wall between the kitchen and the living room. Know what I mean? Opening it up to glass doors and a large deck. Lots of light and space." Putting her fork down, Jan spread her hands outward to suggest the enlarged space. "The new kitchen island would act as a natural wall, so to speak, between the two rooms."

Cole watched Jan's hands as they moved to mimic the internal architecture of a structure unknown to her. As hard as she tried, Cole couldn't visualize the house. But she wasn't really listening. Only watching, wondering what had gone wrong. Why they'd broken up. She had tried time and time again to pinpoint what exactly had happened. Three years and a house after they had met, Jan announced she needed her space. It was sudden and it was devastating. Cole had done her best to take it in stride, to be understanding, to accept Jan's needs. She even began packing, filling her car's trunk with flattened U-Haul boxes to complete the tedious process ahead. Then the next startling announcement had been made.

"Cole, what in the world are you doing?"

Cole shoved her hands in her pockets. "Uh, packing."

Jan was standing in the foyer, sunlight from the window above streaking her dark hair with golden highlights. She shook her head and pursed her lips. "You don't have to leave."

Cole stared at Jan, then at the boxes she had dragged in from the back alley. "But you said you needed space."

Jan started to tap her foot. The hollow sound of her shoe hitting the hardwood floor echoed in Cole's ears. "This is where we have our problems, you know. You don't listen."

Dropping her head, Cole suddenly had a view of her boots. They were scuffed and faded. She needed a new pair. "I was listening," she mumbled.

"Well, then you know that I just need a little space from our relationship right now. Look at me." Jan rested her hand on Cole's shoulder. "That doesn't mean you have to leave. It just means that I need to meet new people. See if this is what's right for me."

Cole stepped backward. "If I'm right for you?" Impatience had crept into her voice. She felt on edge. "Maybe you'll find someone better?"

"Damn, Cole. It's not always about you, you know."

"Sure seems like it is."

The blue eyes flashed at her through an angry squint. "If you loved me, you'd understand."

"I do love you and I'm trying to understand. Honest I am."

"Then just let things be for now, okay?"

"What's really happened? Find someone else?"

"Oh God, Cole. That's just like you."

"That's not an answer."

"No. I haven't found anyone else. It's just me I'm trying to find."

So Cole had put the boxes in the cellar, wondering as she stacked them across from the laundry chute what the sleeping arrangements were going to be. Would she end up on the futon in the den? Sure enough, the ceiling in the den became the surface she bounced her thoughts from. So, what's wrong with me? she lay thinking. What did she do to cause this? Was there really someone else? Was Jan having a mid-thirties crisis? Night after night she talked to the ceiling, but the ceiling threw her words back until, maddeningly, she understood no more than she had before. Finally, she stopped asking questions and decided to wait out Jan's passing phase — to be understanding and loving and supportive. Still, she wondered how long she'd have to wait, how long she could wait.

The worst torture was knowing Jan lay thirty feet away down a short hallway behind the door that used to be their bedroom. Many evenings, in the darkness and quiet, Cole imagined making love to Jan until her heart raced with the memories and there were no walls, hallways or doors between them. She could almost feel Jan's whispered breaths against her cheek and the taut fingers pressing into her back. In her sleep, too, she loved her — waking up in a sweat of passion, fully aroused. Her first thought was always, "Walls and doors be damned." But she never made it more than halfway down the hall.

Long, sleep-deprived nights of lovemaking with Jan had not always been a dream or distant memory. Cole remembered their first night together in Jan's old apartment near Washington Square. Coats, clothes, shoes were discarded in heaps on the bedroom floor. Cole kissed the smooth skin on Jan's neck and then pressed against her, feeling the warmth of their bodies and the heat of their kisses. She stroked Jan's hair and touched her cheek, then kissed her again and caressed her breasts. Her nipples were hard and she teased them lightly with her fingers. Jan sighed deeply as Cole took a firm nipple into her mouth, flicking it with her tongue. Jan moved beneath her with soft responsive cries. She filled her mouth with Jan's breasts, then moved down to kiss her stomach and stroke her thighs.

Jan whispered into her ear, "Fuck me." The words startled her, but aroused her at the same time. The firm thighs parted and she stroked the wetness lovingly. Jan's own thrusts pushed her deeper inside. Cole kissed her hips and then straddled her, forcing one hand with the other to follow Jan's frantic movements.

"I love you," she whispered against Jan's stomach.

Jan dug her fingers into Cole's shoulders as she came, her body twitching and arching as it satisfied itself. Cole could feel the orgasm come with hard contractions, then ebb away as Jan finally settled back, her rapid breaths still audible, tears streaming down her face.

Cole had eased her hand slowly from between Jan's thighs and held her close, kissing her forehead and whispering, "Baby, I love you. I love you."

Suddenly, dinner was over and Cole was jolted back to the present. Jan walked around the table to collect her plate. The warmth of Jan next to her made her skin tingle. A few minutes later, they stood side by side, Jan scraping the dishes, Cole dropping them into the dishwasher.

Jan handed her a fork. "You never told me about your day. You said it was crazy. That's all."

For a brief moment, Cole held both the fork and the hand that passed it to her. Then she let go. "Uh, I covered that accident downtown. You hear about it?"

"Someone was killed."

Cole cleared her throat. "Yes. Big mess. Gotta head downstairs and do some work." She coughed and blinked back tears, which had come without warning.

Jan patted her on the back. "You all right?"

Flashing a smile, Cole wiped her eyes with the sleeve of her shirt. "Fine. Chicago street dirt."

Snapping the plastic lids shut, Jan slid the Tupperware containers into the refrigerator. "Listen, I'm running out to the support group tonight. Shouldn't be too late."

Spontaneously, Cole grunted. For months, Jan had been attending a lesbian support group sponsored by the Chicago Gay and Lesbian Center. Cole had tried to be encouraging, but now it was starting to irk her. It seemed that Jan needed the support group more than she needed her. She poured some soap into the dishwasher and closed the door. When Cole looked up, Jan was standing with hands on hips, foot tapping, mouth tightened into a stubborn line.

"Why the grunt?"

"Uh, nothing. Just forgot it's Wednesday. Support group night."

"I know you don't approve, but I think it's doing me a lot of good."

"I never said I didn't approve."

"You don't have to."

"Okay, I'm sorry. That was rude. You guys doing something special?"

"Yes. Actually, it's a bit of a field trip. We're going down to Navy Pier to see a show. Just for the hell of it."

"Sounds like fun," Cole said neutrally.

"Should be." Jan ambled down the hallway to her bedroom. "Have to quick change. See you later. Don't work too hard."

Standing in the blackness of her darkroom, Cole fastened her brown leather apron and opened film cans. Loading the unexposed film onto plastic reels, she finally felt safe. The darkroom was an escape from the rest of the world. In here it was only her, the chemicals and the equipment. Time stopped and she was able to lose herself in her work.

She placed the film reels into the light-tight canisters filled with developer and turned on the overhead light. While she agitated the film, she studied the prints from this morning's subway murder hanging above her head. One of the photographs showed the outline of a body covered by a police tarp. A trail of blood ran from the body's torso onto the concrete surface of the subway tunnel. In another photograph, splattered footprints of blood led south down the tunnel until the blood had worn from the bottom of the assailant's shoes, fading into indiscernible smears. They were good photos, she thought.

Her darkroom was traditional in every way. There were new digital darkrooms where everything was computerized, where photo editing was done with pressure-sensitive drawing tablets and sophisticated software that managed composition and the size of the image. Even the *Trib* was looking into the benefits of digital systems. At a conference not long ago, she had talked to a wedding and studio photographer who had just converted to digital processing.

"Hell, in every damned photo I'd taken of this one bride and groom, the groom had his eyes closed. Ordinarily, I would've yanked my hair out. But with the digital equipment, I was able to scan a recent photo of the groom, remove his eyes from that photo and paste them into the other photos. Saved me an entire job."

"But isn't that kind of cheating?" Cole asked.

"No, it's saving your ass."

Regardless of the technical advantages, Cole had clung steadfastly to the old ways. Trays of chemicals were lined up in front of her. Each print was exposed and developed by hand, rinsed in a water bath, squeegeed and then put through a print dryer. The smell of the chemicals, the feel of the paper, the sound of running water made her forget the world outside.

She worked for almost two more hours, developing the prints from the afternoon car wreck. The pungent smell of the chemicals was still on her hands when she finally dried the last of the prints and put them in an envelope ready for delivery to the paper.

From Irving Park, Cole took Lake Shore Drive south to Michigan Avenue, better known to tourists as the Magnificent Mile. The *Chicago Tribune* offices were located in the famous Tribune Tower. The design of the Tribune Tower was the result of an international competition for the "most beautiful office building in the world" held in 1922 by the newspaper. Cole gazed up at the top of the building with its crowning tower and flying buttresses derived from the French cathedral of Rouen. In bright daylight or full moonlight, the building cast a striking silhouette.

The base of the building was studded with over 120 stones from famed sites and structures in all 50 states and dozens of foreign countries. Cole had been amazed to learn, when she first started working for the paper, that the building actually bore pieces of the Parthenon, the Great Wall of China and the Taj Mahal.

At the security desk, Cole flashed her badge and hopped onto an elevator, punching the button for the fifth floor. It was ten before eleven and the place was a zoo. Reporters, artists, columnists and administrative personnel were scattered throughout the large room, working at computers, faxing documents, talking on the phone and milling at the door to the break room. Many of them smiled, waved and said hello as she passed. She walked through the double doors at the rear of the large, open area and through another set of doors to the photo lab. Marty was at his desk checking a stack of proofs.

"Hey, Marty. Where's Donna? Got the photos for her to scan."

"Cole, I was getting worried." Marty sneezed into a crumpled tissue. His face was pockmarked and worn, like the sole of an old Army boot. "She's with Barnes. They're waiting for you. Better get moving." He mockingly shooed her out of the room.

"Oh, okay." Cole backtracked through both sets of double doors. Jerry Barnes was the local news editor and had an office halfway down the open room on the right. Through the glass window, she could see both Barnes and Donna hovering over the computer. Cole thumped her fist on the door once and strode into the office. "Evening. Marty said you were waiting for these."

Barnes took an unlit cigar from his mouth. He chomped on the things constantly. "Yes, we've been waiting for them and you."

Cole looked at her watch and smiled. "Hey, I've got four minutes to spare."

"Let's have 'em." Barnes stuck his arm out and snapped his fingers. Cole handed him the envelope. Tearing into it, Barnes eyed the prints quickly. He looked up at her, then glanced through them again, this time more slowly. "Damn, this is good work," he said at a low mumble.

"What?" Cole asked.

Barnes shrugged, an improvised smile crossing his face. It was rare for him to smile, even if it was forced. "Some things are worth waiting for, Evans. You do good work." He placed one of the photos on the scanner. "You do damned good work."

"Thanks. Sorry if I kept you waiting."

"Hey, no problem. Wanna stick around? This is front-page stuff."

Cole declined and it was just after midnight when she got home. Jan was still out with her friends. She made a cup of hot chocolate and settled into the sofa to watch a late-show movie on television, an old Sidney Poitier flick called *A Patch of Blue*. Poitier's character stumbles across a blind girl in a park, befriends her and helps her get enrolled in a school for the blind. He tells her that she's living in the "dark ages" because she can't read Braille or dial a telephone. Cole decided right then and there, as she watched the school bus pull away from the curb at movie's end, that this was her "dark age." She loved her work, cared about her friends, felt connected to the house, was inspired by the city. But without Jan solidly in her life, she felt as though she had lost one of her major senses. She didn't like living on the fringes of love. Be there or don't be there, she thought. What puzzled her was how to step down to the next lowest rung on the ladder without looking down and feeling as miserable as she expected to feel.

The front door flew open and the depressing view of the imaginary ladder suddenly vanished. Jan took off her coat and shivered, rubbing her hands together to stimulate blood flow.

"It's freezing out there! Invigorating though." Jan laughed when she saw Cole balled up on the sofa with an old afghan wrapped around her shoulders. "You look miserable."

Funny, I was just feeling that way, too, she thought. "It's cold in here. We must need a new furnace or something."

"No." Jan giggled. "It's Chicago and it's ten degrees outside." Jan threw two more logs on the fire and sat down on the edge of the sofa behind Cole. The closeness made the chill leave Cole — and suddenly her heart ached with an inner longing. "Sorry I'm late," Jan said, massaging Cole's shoulders. "God, our group's never gone on this long!" Jan sighed and then yawned loudly. "Can't believe it's almost two in the morning. Thank God I don't have any early appointments tomorrow. Sometimes we can get so downright silly we forget why we're even a group. I like those nights, you know?" Leaning forward, Jan brushed the hair away from Cole's eyes. She squeezed Cole's shoulders playfully. "There's a time to be serious. But we need to have some fun, too."

"Fun is a good thing," Cole agreed, trying to ignore the touch of Jan's fingers. She convinced herself that the backrub was an absent-minded act. Jan had always massaged her shoulders and played with her hair while they talked, made love, drove around in the car.

"After Navy Pier and the show, we went over to Diamond's house."

"Diamond?"

"Yeah, just a nickname." Jan chuckled. "As in 'diamond in the rough.'"

Cole nodded. "Oh. I get it."

"Her real name's Evelyn. Lover left her with two kids. They're adorable. When we got to her house, the babysitter had already put them to bed. We snuck into their room to see them. Cute as anything! Two girls, five and seven."

"Two kids. A lot to handle."

"Yeah, but Diamond's got her act pretty much together. After spying on the kids, we sat and blabbed for hours, drinking virgin margaritas. Killer stuff — even without the alcohol. What have you been doing?"

"Uh, nothing much. Watching an old movie. Glad you had so much fun tonight."

"Thanks. Listen, you look tired."

"I'm not really. Although I should be after the day I had."

"Go to bed." Jan kissed Cole's cheek. "See you in the morning."

Cole grabbed Jan's hand and turned around to face her. Holding her hand tightly, she said, "Earlier this evening, when I started to say that I missed something. Uh, what I really wanted to say was that I missed us." Inwardly, Cole cringed. She felt the ladder swaying in the wind. She had one foot precariously balanced on a rung and the other dangling in the cold breeze — headed one way or the other, up or down.

Jan smiled politely, her blue eyes vibrant in the lamplight. "I knew what you were trying to say. You made a decent recovery, but I was already onto you, I'm afraid."

"Sorry."

"Don't be. You need to say what you're feeling more often."

"Uh, I try. But I don't want to pressure you. I don't want you to think that making love to you is all I care about. It's us being together. Having fun, doing things as a couple like we used to."

"I understand, Cole, and I don't feel pressured.

You've been very patient. But you've got to be fair to your own feelings, too."

Fair? All's fair in love and support groups? Cole pulled Jan closer. Her heart hammered in her ears as she whispered, "I want to kiss you right now. Hold you in my arms until morning."

Jan rested her head on Cole's shoulder. "I'm not ready for that. As tempting as it is, I still need more time."

Cole kissed Jan's cheek and then, reluctantly, let go of her hand. Dangling limply from her imaginary ladder, she stiffened and hit the rung below. Going down, she thought. Going down. "Just wanted you to know I still love you," she said, trying to mask her disappointment and hurt.

"Thank you. That was very sweet." Jan turned out the lamp. "Now, go to bed. You're going to be exhausted tomorrow. I don't have an appointment until eleven, but I need to get some rest myself. Good night."

"Good night."

Lying in the dark on the futon, Cole found peace uneasily. She tossed and turned, at odds with her feelings. Feelings of rejection and a terrible, aching loneliness. She didn't want to feel this way. Didn't want to feel any of it. Finally she slid one of the pillows over her head. The dark ages of her new life with Jan faded into a dark dream until she remembered nothing at all.

Chapter Two

The next morning Cole didn't have time to think about how tired she was. Just out of the shower, she was beeped immediately to cover a murder scene.

The house was stately, a Victorian-style structure dating back to the late 1940s, Cole thought. She stood midway across the street, trying to encapsulate the bustling scene into the camera's viewfinder. They were bringing the body out now. The gurney bumped heavily down the steps, jostling the body beneath the white sheet. Cole shot four or five frames, then jogged closer to the ambulance. She snapped a few more frames of the body being loaded into the vehicle and she was finished.

She had overheard the cops talking about the victim — an older woman in her late sixties. Shot several times in the chest, she was already dead when the authorities arrived. The call to the scene had been made by the woman's niece, who was standing on the steps just outside the front door. She was tall, about five foot eleven, and very thin — almost frail-looking. Cole estimated that she was in her early to mid-forties. She had long, red hair — wavy and unruly. And dark eyes like a bird of prey.

Cole stepped onto the curb and dropped her backpack to the sidewalk. She began to stow her equipment, removing the wide-angle lens from the camera and slipping it into its velvet-lined case. When she looked up, the woman with the flyaway red hair was standing in front of her. She lit a cigarette and glared at Cole, the long thin line of exhaled smoke disappearing into the breeze.

"You with the press or somethin'?"

Cole slung her bag over her shoulder. "Yes."

"Thought so. No one else'd be takin' pictures of a dead woman."

Cole noticed the harsh attitude at the same time she noticed the Southern accent. It was a pronounced drawl that surprised her because it certainly wasn't commonplace in downtown Chicago. The woman was neatly dressed in pressed blue jeans, Western-style boots and an expensive-looking black leather jacket. The jacket was unzipped to just below the breast revealing a striped denim shirt. Not dressed for the cold weather, she stood rigidly, one hand shoved deep into her jacket pocket, the other holding the cigarette between her thumb and forefinger. "Sorry about your loss," Cole said.

"Thanks. I'm Tracy. Tracy Roberts. But people who know me call me Tray. Nickname I've had since I was a kid."

She stuck out her hand and Cole shook it. In addition to being cold, it was also rough and callused. "Cole Evans. I work for the *Chicago Tribune*. Freelance photographer."

"Must be interestin' work."

Cole stared at the face. Sepia-toned, it was heavily lined and leathery from overexposure to the sun. There was barely the hint of a smile and, under the present circumstances, Cole understood why. Still, there was an attractiveness about Tray's features that overcame the hard look. "It can be." Cole cocked her head toward the house. "Do you know what happened?"

The falcon-like gaze was searching, as if for answers, until it finally rested on Cole again. "Was out for a while. Next thing ya know, I'm back at the house callin' the cops." Tray flicked her cigarette into the street.

"I'm sorry."

"My aunt was lyin' facedown on the kitchen floor. I rolled her over, saw she wasn't breathin' and started CPR. Yelled for help, but no one came." Tray took a pack of cigarettes out of her leather jacket. "Had to stop CPR long enough to dial nine-one-one."

"What do the cops think?"

"Maybe a robbery. Someone desperate for money to buy drugs. Strange to have somethin' like this happen in broad daylight." The end of Tray's new cigarette flared red. "But that's the big city for you."

"It can be dangerous."

"I'm from a small town," Tray said, her eyes shifting back toward the street. "This big city thing's new to me."

"Where you from?"

"The hills of Kentucky, honey. A long ways from here." Tray let out a hoarse laugh that stuck in the back of her throat. "Must say I'm havin' quite a time gettin' used to you Yanks."

Cole flashed a conspiratorial smile. "We're not so bad once you get to know us. Honest. How'd you end up in Chicago, anyway?"

"Lived in Atlanta for the last couple years. After years of sweat, I'd finally gotten my medical degree and had been workin' at a hospital there. Finished my residency, then got a temporary fellowship in the trauma unit. That is, until about six months ago when this crazy-ass woman rams into my truck because she wasn't payin' attention to where the hell she was goin'." She took a long drag on her cigarette. "Broad-sided me on the driver's side. Since then, haven't been able to work. Came here to live with my aunt for a while 'til I could get my life straightened out." She looked back at the house. "Now this."

"Sounds like you've had some tough breaks recently."

"Yeah. But I keep pickin' myself right back up. What else can you do, honey?"

"Not much." Cole felt her beeper vibrate. She snapped it from her belt and checked the number. It was the newspaper. "Hey, sorry. Have to get moving here."

Tray's long face forced another smile. "That's okay. Gotta get to the hospital and look after my aunt. Except for my son, she was the only family I had left."

"I'm sorry. Listen, you take care, okay?"

"Yeah, sure. You, too." Tray walked slowly back toward the house, her gait lethargic and heavy-footed.

Cole felt a pang of remorse and started to call after her. But Tray was a stranger and there was little she could do for her. As she sped down the street in her Honda, she glanced one last time at the house and saw Tray wave good-bye from the top step.

There was one tradition of togetherness that Cole and Jan had not abandoned. Once a month, on a Saturday morning, they visited the University of Chicago's Children's Hospital to entertain the ambulatory children who were recovering from operations, having drug or physical therapy, dialysis and other treatments. Jan brought her flute and Cole hauled a huge box of magic tricks and *Sesame Street* puppets.

Dr. Harold Taylor met them in the center's lobby. He was a nationally renowned nephrologist who worked out of the University of Chicago Hospitals and Health System, but who was often called to consult on difficult cases in other parts of the country.

"Cole, Jan, great to see you. The kids are waiting anxiously as usual."

"How are you, Doctor?" Cole asked, lugging her sack filled with surprises.

"Busy, as always. But never too busy to greet the two of you and thank you once again for being here," the doctor replied in a gruff but friendly voice.

"We love these kids," Jan said. "Wouldn't miss the chance to brighten their day a little if we can."

When they entered the large room of the center, the children were already waiting, sitting in metal chairs lined up in rows. Some of the children had rolled their wheelchairs into position, and along the walls most of the curtains were drawn so that the children receiving dialysis could also see the show.

They were greeted with cheers and enthusiastic applause. Jan immediately unpacked her flute and began to play the *Sesame Street* theme song. The kids laughed and clapped as Cole staged her puppet show and, when it was over a half-hour later, Cole pulled out her bag of magic tricks. With the hospital's permission, she had brought a live rabbit to pull out of her black top hat. The rabbit was a friend's pet and more than willing to curl up in the top portion of the hat where it was warm and cozy. When Cole tapped the empty hat and pulled out the live rabbit, the youngsters squealed with delight. Cole walked around the room, allowing the children to see the rabbit.

In the meantime, Jan went from curtain to curtain to play tunes for the children undergoing dialysis. The children absolutely beamed, forgetting for a short while why they were there. One boy told Jan it was his birthday. She played "Happy Birthday" and all the children joined in, singing loudly.

As Cole was packing up her equipment and the rabbit, she felt a tug on her belt loop. She turned to find the prettiest little red-haired girl, no older than five.

"May I pet the bunny?" she asked in a high-pitched squeak.

"You sure can, honey," Cole said, sitting down on the floor. At that level, Cole and the freckle-faced girl were about even height.

"What's the bunny's name?"

"Snowball," Cole said. "What's your name?"

"Jackie."

"Hi, Jackie." Cole cradled the bunny in her hands. "Here, you can pet him."

Jackie patted the bunny on the head. The rabbit winced and blinked, its nose wiggling.

"Is the bunny sick like us?"

"No. The bunny's just fine. How are you feeling today?"

"Better. I come here twice a week. But maybe, someday, Mommy says I won't have to come no more."

"Well, I hope that's true."

"You're funny. You made us laugh," she said, bending down. With her hands on her knees, she kissed Cole on the forehead. "Thank you, lady. For bringing the bunny and the show."

"You're welcome." There was a lump in Cole's throat the size of Lake Michigan. Jackie turned and hopped away, in an imitation of the rabbit.

"I think you've got a fan there," Jan said, putting her hand on Cole's shoulder.

Chapter Three

On Monday, Cole received a message on her voice mail that her boss, Sheila Anderson, wanted to have lunch with her. Their luncheon meetings were a bimonthly ritual Cole could sometimes do without. But overall, she liked working for Sheila and was willing to endure these informal meetings, if only for the benefit of the free lunch.

"I've been very impressed with your work, Cole. Right from the beginning." Sheila Anderson, senior editor for the *Chicago Tribune*, brushed the bangs of her silver hair away from her face. "You know that's true. And I've certainly tried to communicate that to you over the past couple of years."

"You have, Sheila. And I appreciate it very much."

"Good. Now, I have a proposition for you."

Cole squirted some ketchup onto her fries and almost onto her lap. It had been some time since a woman had propositioned her, she joked to herself. "Oh? What's that?"

"I'd like you to consider full-time status at the paper. If you accept, there would be an increase in salary, of course." Sheila glanced at her, then pushed her glasses down over her nose, waiting for some kind of response.

Cole nodded. She had heard this proposal before and had never given it much thought. But now she listened with renewed interest. "I guess we were destined to have this talk again."

Sheila laid her glasses on the table. "We certainly were, Cole. I want you on staff with a great organization to back your work. And you'd be eligible for full benefits." Taking a sip of her Coke, Sheila leaned forward in her chair. "You're very talented. The work you do is top-notch. Won't you please consider a formal offer? I'll have one drawn up immediately."

Cole had always been flattered by Sheila's confidence in her work. In the past her hesitancy to accept any full-time offers from the paper had been grounded in her fierce independence. No office politics, no hours set in stone. These were freedoms she had learned to enjoy. And, most importantly, no compromise of the high standards she set for the quality of her work. The work she delivered every day in an envelope to the *Trib* was the work she chose to deliver . . . and nothing less. Cole had felt pressured in the past —

more so because she liked Sheila and appreciated her praise as well as her constructive criticisms. Now there were other pressures as well. Would she have to move into her own place soon? Buy her own home? If that were the case, she would need the extra money and benefits. Cole shifted nervously in her chair and cleared her throat. "Can I have more time to think about it, Sheila? I'm so grateful for your confidence in me, but I think it'd be hard for me to work under different conditions."

Sheila laughed and made a half-hearted stab at her salad. "You like being your own boss. I can understand that, believe me." She shook her head. "Don't think I don't understand the downside of working in an office environment — office politics, the backstabbing — but I honestly think the good far outweighs the bad."

Cole shrugged helplessly. "Maybe," she conceded.

"Listen, while you work for me, nobody's going to dog your every footfall. I'll promise you as much independence as I can within the boundaries of the paper's policies. I'm not the kind of boss that breathes down people's necks. You know that."

"I'll think about it. Honestly, I will."

"Promise?"

"Promise." Cole forced a smile and took a bite of her hamburger. With her mouth full, she felt certain that Sheila wouldn't attempt to extract any further assurances.

That evening, Cole was happy to be staring at the still-boyish smile of her best friend, Jackson Ward. His emerald green eyes were piercing in the firelight. Running his fingers through his sandy blond hair, he poured the rest of Cole's beer into a pilsner glass. "You really ought to go full-time at the paper," he said, handing her the beer. "I think it would be a smart move."

They were seated in one of Cole's favorite restaurants, Printer's Row, located in what was known as the "Printer's Row" district downtown. Once a dilapidated area, the neighborhood was now upscale with completely renovated buildings, loft apartments and new businesses.

The menu offered was American, and the game and seafood dishes were rated very highly. One of Cole's favorite entrees was seared scallops.

"I know, I know. I'm going to give it some serious thought, trust me. I just may take Sheila up on her offer this time."

"You need to think about your future." Jackson sipped his Chardonnay and smiled, swirling the gold liquid in the glass. "Which brings up another point. If you take the job full-time at the paper, you can get your own place and be happy again."

Cole felt suddenly defensive. "You think I'm unhappy?"

Jackson placed his free hand over hers and squeezed gently. "Cole, you've been unhappy ever since Jan decided to go on her 'vision quest.' Maybe it's time to walk away and start a new life for yourself."

She looked at Jackson and her lips suddenly trembled. He was like a brother to her. They had been friends for as long as she could remember, had lived on the same street, gone to the same grammar school and high school. Suffered the trials and tribulations of coming out to their families — his with drastic results. She counted on him to tell her the truth and he just had.

"It's going to be okay. I know you still love her. But you've got to start preparing yourself for what might happen." Jackson sunk his chin into his hand and grimaced. "Easier said than done. I'm full of shit tonight, aren't I?"

"No. I need to hear this stuff. You know I'm already thinking about it anyway."

"Of course you are. Any sane person would be."

"Sometimes I don't feel so sane. I'm questioning my self-worth constantly. All because Jan's on this search for inner nirvana or something." Disgusted, Cole drowned a steamed clam in melted butter. "I understand that people go through these phases. But I can't help feeling sometimes like she's keeping me around and pushing me away at the same time. And you know me. I'm not one to wear out my welcome."

"I think you need to have a fling."

Cole laughed until her sides hurt. "Are you making an offer?"

"You'd be the only woman I'd make one to, I can assure you," Jackson said with a mischievous wink. "I'm serious. Why don't *you* attempt nirvana? A healthy sexual fling can get you there pretty quickly."

"Not a bad idea. It's been quite a while since nirvana and I have made our acquaintance. As in six months a while."

"No wonder you're moody and depressed." Jackson slid the assorted appetizer plate closer to Cole.

Cole helped herself to a fried cheese stick. "Moody? Depressed? Thanks a lot, my friend."

"Not true?"

"Okay, true. Listen, I'll make a deal with you."

"What's that?"

"I'll think hard about my future with the paper — and maybe I'll even have a fling. But only on one condition."

"Condition?" Jackson rubbed his chin thoughtfully. "Hmmm. What are you thinking?"

"I'll do all that if you stop cruising those horrible bars and settle down with your own new love. How about that?"

Jackson shrugged and popped a deep-fried mushroom into his mouth. "You know, there's always food. Neither one of us has to put our hearts on the line. We can just eat until we bust. Hell, you know food can be even better than sex."

"Nice way to avoid the issue, my friend. But not a bad idea, I have to admit. In fact, I think I'll order a slice of that chocolate cheesecake I had the last time we were here." Cole flipped the menu over and scrutinized the list of desserts.

"Before or after dinner?"

"Oh, that'll be after I order the swordfish special."

"What? No large dinner salad?"

"Jackson, I don't think I'm going to order anything remotely green or healthy for a long time." She pushed the menu to the side. "Besides, that's why I had you bring me here. So I could eat something wonderful. Large dinner salads are reserved for when you take me to a chain."

Jackson asked playfully, "When do I ever take you to a chain restaurant?"

"Far too often."

Friday had finally arrived and Cole looked forward to the weekend. As she slowly climbed the stairs to the upstairs foyer, she envisioned sleeping late tomorrow and then lingering over the morning paper.

Cole could hear voices in the living room even before she entered. Weighed down with camera equipment and stacks of old file photos, she pushed the door open with her hip and stumbled into the room, dropped the camera bag to the floor and slid the backpack from her shoulders. The backpack caught on one of the file folders she was holding underneath her arm and sent a mosaic of black and white prints across the carpet. She cursed under her breath and heard laughter coming from the adjoining room.

"Can I help you?" a voice said.

Kneeling on the floor, Cole looked up into the face of a total stranger. "Uh, hi there. Who are you?" she asked, forcing a smile.

The woman bent down and started to pick up some of the photos. "Name's Shaun. I'm in Jan's support group. You must be Cole," she said with a tentative smile.

Cole stuffed some prints into a folder. "Yes, I'm Cole. Nice to meet you."

"Man, I've seen your work in the *Trib*. Gosh, you're good."

Cole glanced at her. She looked young, maybe

twenty-five. Dark brown hair, accented by purple bangs, framed an attractive face. Her lower lip was pierced with a prominent silver ring. "Thanks for the compliment."

"You're welcome." Shaun handed Cole the last of the photos. "Want to join us? We're just sipping some wine and being stupid."

"Uh, thanks, but I've got a lot of work to do," Cole lied. She got up and piled the manila folders onto the dining room table. "Say, where's Jan?"

"In the kitchen. Man, we got hungry — so she's making us a snack." Shaun smiled broadly, the silver ring in her lip flopping with every word. "Whenever I start talking about my ex-girlfriends, all I can think about is food."

Cole wondered how many ex-girlfriends this young woman could possibly have. Then she cringed inwardly, imagining Jan talking about *her* — giving personal details about *their* relationship. She felt queasy. "No doubt," she finally mumbled. "Again, it was nice meeting you."

"Hey, right. Cool meeting you, too."

Cole bolted for the kitchen. Jan was hovering over the counter slicing Muenster cheese. "Evening," Cole said abruptly. "Didn't know we were having company tonight."

Jan spun around and smiled. "Cole! I was getting worried. You're late." Jan hugged her tightly, then kissed her cheek. "Oh, you're cold. Ears red as beets. You should take a nice warm bath and relax."

"Sounds like a good idea."

"But first you have to meet the ladies."

"Is Wednesday now Friday?"

"What?"

"Your support group. It's Friday. Why are they here?"

"Oh, it's just sort of an impromptu thing." She grabbed Cole's arm. "C'mon, I want you to meet them."

"Wait. I don't think that's a good idea." Leaning against the refrigerator, Cole felt one of the magnets poke her in the back.

"Why not?" Jan asked, annoyed.

Jan stood with her hands on her hips. She was dressed in a gray wool sweater and black slacks. Cole blinked, trying to concentrate her thoughts somewhere else — anywhere but on those hips curving down . . . "Uh, I'd feel funny. I think."

"What are you talking about? They've been wanting to meet you for months."

Cole averted her eyes, glancing up at the drop ceiling she'd meant to tear out months ago. "Just would. Feel funny, I mean."

The pitch of Jan's voice rose slightly. "These are my friends, Cole. I'd like you to meet them."

"I can appreciate that. But it's like . . . uh, like walking naked into a crowd of people. They know all about me. I don't know anything about them." Cole looked at Jan. Her face was flushed. She was angry and beautiful at the same time. Damn her. "Uh, except Shaun. The one with the pierced lip."

"I know who Shaun is, Cole." Jan threw her hands up in disgust. "I haven't told them anything bad about you. Mostly, I talk about myself and the confusion I'm feeling within me. I'm the one who's lost. It's not always about you. Nor is it always your fault."

"Uh, okay. But listen, they're your friends and I'd feel like an intruder. And, I've really got a lot of work to do —"

"Fine!" she said. "That's just fine! Do whatever makes you happy." Jan brushed by her and started slicing cheese again.

Cole quietly opened the basement door and hurried down the steps two at a time. She rounded the corner to the darkroom and slipped inside, the word *fine* still echoing unpleasantly in her ears.

Chapter Four

Cole hated Mondays, especially when they started with a staff meeting. The meeting was running long, which was not at all unusual. One more reason she liked being an independent contractor. This was the only weekly meeting she was required to attend, yet she caught herself fidgeting, her left knee bouncing up and down, the papers in her hands now rolled into a tube. She began tapping the tube on her thigh until Deb, the woman sitting next to her, flashed her a look of annoyance. Cole smiled and stopped tapping. She hated meetings of any kind. What was said in an hour could always be said in five minutes or, better yet, a three-line e-mail. The door to her right opened and a head popped in. It was Rita, one of the administrative secretaries for the department.

"Cole," she whispered, cracking her gum in Cole's ear. "Phone call for you."

Deb flashed her another dirty look. Cole shot up out of her chair, realizing that the phone call was the perfect excuse for escaping the rest of the meeting. She slunk through the door and into the hallway.

"I'll transfer it to that empty cube over there," Rita pointed.

"Hey, thanks." Cole sat down at the desk and played with the levers attached to the swivel chair until she was comfortable. A few seconds later the phone rang. "Cole Evans."

"Hey, baby."

Even though she had only heard the voice on one prior occasion, it was unmistakable. "Tray Roberts?"

"Ah, you remembered. But I knew you were a smart woman the first moment I laid eyes on you."

"Your voice is like a fingerprint."

"It helps that this is Chicago and not Kentucky," Tray answered with a hoarse laugh. "How are you, honey?"

"Just fine. Can I help you with something in particular?"

Tray laughed again. "So, you want to know why I'm callin'. All business, you are."

"Uh, well, I am at work."

"Of course you are. The paper was the only way I could track you down. Like to have a drink with me tonight?"

Cole paused. She could hear Tray lighting a

cigarette. She didn't know why she was hesitating. After all, there would be no one at home tonight waiting for her. "Sure, why not?"

"Great! Meet me at The River. Know where?"

"Yes, I've been there a time or two."

"Good. Just remember to smile real pretty when you walk in the door. That way, I'll be sure to see you no matter how crowded the place is."

"Uh, yes. I'm sure you'll find me. Six okay?"

"Any time that's good for you honey is good for me."

They said their good-byes and then later that evening, Cole strolled into The River, a restaurant that derived its name from its location along the shoreline of the Chicago River. The restaurant was known not only for its food, but also as a "happy-hour" haven. Fighting her way through a sea of people, she eventually spied Tray sitting at the bar, having an animated conversation with the bartender. She was dressed in a smartly tailored, jade-colored suit. Cole hopped up on the seat next to her.

"I've thought about seein' you all day. Thanks for meetin' me tonight, babe."

"Thanks for calling. Say, you're all dressed up. Been out on the town?"

"Business seminar."

"Anything interesting?"

"How to start your own business, marketing tips, that kinda stuff."

Tray ordered Cole a drink, started to talk and barely stopped to take a breath. There was something intriguing about Tray that Cole couldn't quite put her finger on. Cole sipped her frozen lime margarita and listened while Tray continued to talk. From time to time, Tray would tap her lightly on the forearm to emphasize a point. A born storyteller, with her back-woods Southern drawl, she came across as down-to-earth and laid back — a "what you see is what you get" personality. Mostly, she talked about herself and the fact that she was once a "poor kid from Kentucky" born on the "wrong side of the tracks." There was something about Tray's voice — a deep, throaty rumble — that mesmerized Cole. There was something about her story, too, that drew her in. Poor kid from Kentucky makes good — only to lose it all after a debilitating accident.

"Just like that," Tray said, snapping her fingers. "It was all taken away from me in seconds." Anger flashed in her eyes. "Some bitch who's not payin' attention to what she's doin' hits me broadside and blows my career from here to kingdom come. All the work, all the struggles..." she said, her voice trailing off.

"I'm so sorry. What a terrible thing to have happened just when you were getting started with your career."

"Took me years to get through med school. Worked every menial job I could find to get that piece of paper that finally said I was a doctor. Then one crazy bitch takes it all away." Tray rubbed her left shoulder. "It's my shoulder that's shot. I've had six months of rehab. Lost some hearin' in my left ear and have some nerve damage in my left arm and hand. I drop things a lot." There was bitterness in Tray's voice. "Doesn't make for very good suturin' in a hospital trauma unit."

"No, I guess not."

"Also got my teeth knocked out. Before the accident, I'd had 'em all capped, plus brand new implants in the front. First year I worked at the hospital I used all the money I saved to fix this mouth. Still wasn't quite done when the bitch hit me." Tray sipped her drink. "Now my mouth's a fuckin' mess again. Guess you could say, everything in my life's back to normal."

Cole had immediately taken notice of Tray's teeth. From what little she had seen, they were definitely in bad shape. Not only was Tray missing teeth, but there was also visible decay. She noticed that Tray was very self-conscious about smiling. Only when she smiled, were her obvious dental problems revealed.

"I assume you're suing this woman."

"Yeah. For all my injuries, including the teeth. Just hope I can wait that long. It's pretty damned embarrassin'." Clearly wanting to change the subject, Tray said, "Know how I saved enough money to start college?"

Cole shifted on the barstool, steeling herself for another story. "How?"

"Worked in the coal mines. I was the first fuckin' woman coal miner in the state of Kentucky." Tray lit another cigarette. Talking through the smoke, she said, "Amazin' I wasn't killed in the mines long before I ever made it to UK."

Cole was suddenly impressed. "Wow, you went to UK? UK's a great school."

"Yep. Made it through on a woman's basketball scholarship. What I lacked in talent I made up for in sheer guts and determination."

"Well, you had height on your side," Cole observed, looking her up and down. Even seated, her height was obvious. About five foot eleven, Cole guessed.

"Yeah, but I hated it," she declared with a wave of her hand. "The whole playin' basketball for the right to be there thing. But it got me where I wanted to be. Sometimes, it just felt too much like a job. I'd have given it up in a heartbeat but couldn't."

"What did you do after college?"

"You mean before I decided to be a doctor?"

"Yes."

"First, I worked at a doctor's office. Then I took a six-month class in radiology and ended up workin' as an x-ray technician at a local hospital. That's when I knew I wanted to be a doctor."

"Always knew what I wanted to do. Photography, I mean. Had a passion for it that I inherited from my father."

"What do you like about it?"

"The excitement. The challenge. Always something different happening from one day to the next."

"Know what I liked most about bein' a doctor?" Tray asked, with a faraway look in her eyes.

"What?"

"The kids. It was tough to see them sick or injured from accidents or abuse. But it felt great when I could put 'em back together again." Tray blew a long trail of smoke. Her wild, red hair lay in curls well below her shoulders. "I worked crazy-ass hours. Carried a beeper and a cell phone — even on my days off. Now, I've got to start a whole new career."

Cole wanted to tell Tray her own story about how she entertained kids in the dialysis center once a month, but another question popped into her mind, putting the story on hold. "Can't you teach or something? With a medical degree, I would think you could teach almost anywhere."

"Maybe." Tray's eyes welled with tears and her lips trembled when she talked. "But I don't think so.

It would be too hard for me. Remind me of what I can't do anymore."

"You'll always be a doctor," Cole said, feeling sympathetic. "No one can ever take that away from you."

"No, I'm not a doctor anymore. Have to face facts." Tray slumped in defeat and her brown eyes glistened. "Time to make a new future for myself."

"I'm sure you will."

Tray lit another cigarette and stared at Cole. "Damn, you're awfully pretty."

Cole felt her cheeks flush. "No, I'm definitely not."

"Really. Practically knocked me on my ass when I first saw you."

"You managed to stay on your feet."

"Yeah, but that was the first time I'd ever laid eyes on you. Too soon for compliments." Tray's dark eyes burned into Cole. "You're very pretty, really. Extremely attractive. Beautiful smile, perfect skin . . ."

"Skin that's blushing now because of you. Stop," Cole pleaded.

"Hmmm. Don't take compliments well." Tray drew long and hard on her cigarette. "Inferiority complex? You don't seem the type."

"Well, not really. I don't like to talk about myself much," she said, with a gesture of helplessness. "I'm not a real talker anyway."

"Not like me!" Tray chuckled.

Cole raised her eyebrows and smiled. "Uh, no. Not at all like you."

"Was I boring you with all my sappy stories?"

"No, of course not. You've had a very interesting life. Very, uh, colorful."

Tray slapped the top of the bar with her hand. "Well, babe, that's a new one on me. Colorful."

"Sorry. Didn't mean to offend you."

"No offense taken."

"It just seems like a lot has happened to you. Hell, my life's downright boring compared to yours."

"I've had some rough times, yeah. I'm a mother, too, you know."

"That's right. You mentioned having a son." Cole was curious about Tray's status as a mother. Frankly, she didn't sense anything at all motherly about her. Fatherly maybe. Tray was a stereotypical butch dyke, through and through.

"Yeah, I got married while I was in school. Was young and stupid. Then I got the shit beat outta me once too often and gotta divorce. Have a son named Mark. He's eighteen now."

"Does he live in Chicago?"

"Kentucky. Haven't seen him in over a year. Miss him. My cousin raised him so I could finish college. When I decided to go to med school about eight years ago, Mark just stayed in Kentucky. He didn't want to get yanked around the country and I couldn't blame him. You got any family around the great city of Chicago?"

"No. Both my parents are dead. I have one brother who lives in California. Don't see him much."

"So, you're goin' it alone, then."

"Sort of. Uh, I wanted to ask you, Tray. Did they find out what happened to your aunt? Any suspects or news?"

"Well, they questioned me! Thought maybe I killed her, I guess."

"Oh my God." The thought that Tray might be a suspect had never occurred to Cole.

"Yeah, but it's okay. I was at another seminar when my aunt was murdered. A finance seminar for small business owners. So, I had an alibi and all. Wasn't upset, really. At the cops, I mean. They always have to question the family."

"I'm sorry you had to go through that."

"The worst thing is missing my aunt. Everything else really don't matter much." Tray stubbed out her cigarette. "I'm very attracted to you, Cole. Just want you to know that."

"Uh, thanks." Tray's directness surprised her. "You know, I think I mentioned that I live with my ex right now," Cole blurted. "If you don't know it, you should."

"Only lesbians." Tray shook her head.

"What?"

"Live with their exes. Everybody else has a big fight, storms out, gets separated, divorced, whatever. Not lesbians. We like to torture one another."

"Sometimes it feels that way."

"I hope this doesn't ruin our chances."

"Chances?"

"Of getting to know each other better."

"Why should it?"

"No reason in the world, babe."

On the way home, Cole tried to sort through her feelings about Tray. She had to admit that she felt the spark of an attraction. Still, Tray's past seemed to be filled with potholes that had sent her life careening from one crisis to another. Stability in a relationship had always been important to her — and she wondered if Tray, in the midst of rebuilding her life, could offer that anytime in the near future. Her impressions of

Tray were also muted by Cole's strong feelings for Jan. There was still a hope that she and Jan might work through their problems. And as long as that hope existed, it was hard for her to imagine any other involvement.

Chapter Five

It was difficult getting up early on a Sunday, but Cole had promised Jackson she would help him unpack from his recent move. Saturday and Sunday mornings were the only mornings she slept in, often as late as ten o'clock. Groggily, she extricated herself from the futon and staggered into the kitchen to make a quick cup of coffee. While the coffee brewed, she rushed through a five-minute shower, threw on a pair of jeans and a sweatshirt and stumbled back into the kitchen. She poured the coffee into a travel mug, grabbed her coat and was out the door.

By noon, Cole had worked her way through the dining room and kitchen. She opened one of the last boxes and found the rest of the Mikasa, along with a brand new set of T-fal pots and pans. She finished putting the dishes in the cabinets above the counter. Then she neatly arranged the pots and pans in the cabinets beneath the kitchen island.

"You do such good work, doll." Jackson hopped up on the counter near the sink.

Cole flattened another empty U-Haul box. "Thanks. Hey, I see that guys use U-Haul, too," Cole said, pointing toward the stack of boxes.

Jackson laughed. "Yeah, but not as often as lesbians."

"No, most people have frequent flyer miles. Lesbians have frequent U-Haul miles."

"Hey, that's not a bad promotional idea. U-Haul is one of our clients. I'll have to suggest that angle at the agency."

Jackson had just moved into the Lincoln Park area of the city — a trendy section of restaurants, shops and boutiques. After landing a management job with an advertising firm located about three stops down the metro line, Jackson welcomed the move, along with the career advancement. He was a top-notch artist and illustrator and would now be managing the entire art department for the new company. In the Chicago ad business, he was well known for his artistic talents.

Cole eyed the few boxes that remained in the kitchen. "Well, looks like I'm almost done in here. Just food to put away."

"Appreciate the help, Cole. The guys helped me move the furniture yesterday, you're here helping me today. Hey, I should be settled in pretty quickly."

Jackson was the only gay man Cole knew who didn't obsess over what his apartment looked like. The last time he moved, before he ever knew what Mikasa was, she'd sat on a crate, eating dinner from paper plates.

"Now for the really important news," Jackson said, jumping down from the counter and grabbing Cole's hand. "Sit down for a minute."

"This about the new job?"

"Not exactly."

She sat down on an empty Coleman cooler and studied him. Mr. Cool-as-a-cucumber actually appeared nervous. Beads of sweat appeared on his upper lip. "Wow, this must be some news."

"It is," Jackson said, pacing in front of her. "I think I've finally met Mr. Right."

Cole's mouth flopped open. She blinked several times and couldn't think of a thing to say.

He ran his fingers through his hair. "I know, I know. I can't believe it either. But it's true. Met him last night. The guys and I went out for a beer after we moved the furniture. And there he was, playing pool with some friends." Jackson stopped talking and just stood there looking at her.

"Well, tell me what happened for crying out loud! Don't stop now," she demanded. Jackson had never referred to anyone as Mr. Right and she wanted to hear all the details.

"Okay, okay. Tony, Greg, Hunt and I sat down at the bar. I was tired and not really paying much attention. Greg was the one who said something. He told me he thought this guy at the pool table was checking me out. I ignored him, because Greg is always saying stuff like that. He cruises everyone no matter where we are. We could be at a freaking McDonalds and Greg would give us a running commentary on every guy in the place." Jackson sat down on a box of food. "But for some reason, while I was drinking my beer, I felt this odd sensation that someone was watching me. The little hairs on the back of my neck stood straight up. I glanced toward the pool table and saw him. He was holding a cue stick with both hands, kind of leaning on it. He caught me looking and smiled." Resting his chin in his hands, Jackson continued, dreamily. "The first thing I noticed were his eyes. Dark, dark, dark brown — almost black from that distance. His hair was cut short. Brown with blond highlights."

Cole couldn't stand it anymore. "Did you talk to the guy, or what?"

"He finished his game, then walked over like he wasn't nervous at all. My stomach was churning. He introduced himself. Said, 'Hi, I'm David Tanner, professional pool shark.' Then he laughed and I froze. I was as totally uncool as you could possibly be in a situation like that. Finally he said, 'And you are?' I spit out my name like it was an old wad of gum stuck to the roof of my mouth. It was awful. But he was totally unfazed and kept on talking like I hadn't acted like a jerk at all."

"Sounds like a nice guy."

"I'm meeting him Wednesday night for dinner." Jackson looked at her like a deer caught in headlights. "I can't believe how nervous I am."

"This is unusual for you."

"Yeah, because it really means something. For the first time in a long time, it really means something."

The next morning, when the door opened, Tray stood there with a cigarette dangling from her mouth. It bounced as she talked. "Cole! What a dang nice surprise. My not-so-good day just got a lot better."

Cole looked up at that ubiquitous red hair. It was after eleven o'clock and Tray was still dressed in royal blue silk pajamas. "Was doing a shoot in the area and thought I'd stop by to check on you. I've been worried about you. You're not sick, are you?"

"No. Don't have any appointments today. Mostly been on the phone with lawyers all morning. C'mon in, babe."

Cole stepped into the living room. She almost couldn't believe her eyes. While the outside of the house was attractive and quaint, the inside of the house was in terrible disrepair. The dingy walls were in desperate need of paint, the ceilings were cracked and furnishings worn. There were bulbs dangling from the ceilings without light fixtures. The hardwood floorboards were loose and, in some areas along the walls, missing.

"I know. The place needs a major overhaul. My aunt didn't pay much attention to that kinda thing. What I really need to do is rent a bulldozer and run it through the inside so I can start the fuck all over again."

"Uh, well, it does need some help, that's for sure. Who's in the picture?" Cole pointed to the wall behind the sofa.

"My aunt and my mom. Was taken when they were in high school. My aunt was two years younger than my mom, but they still fought over the same boys."

"They look like sisters."

"Yeah. My aunt was devastated when my mom died. Two years ago of cancer."

"I'm sorry."

"My aunt was really never the same after that. I think she felt like she'd lost the best friend she ever had."

"What about your dad?"

"He died in a car crash when I was little. Don't even remember him."

"So both your parents are gone, too. Just like mine."

"Yeah. Not a good thing to have in common."

"No."

Cole paused at the coffee table. "Wow, this is a gorgeous flower arrangement. Silk, isn't it?"

"That's right. I made it for my aunt as a birthday present. Used to be a hobby of mine."

"Quite a talent."

"Thanks."

The kitchen wasn't in much better shape. Painted puke-green, the room looked straight out of the fifties. Plaster had fallen from the ceiling and many of the linoleum floor tiles had loosened and were stacked in a pile next to the stove.

Tray cleared off the kitchen table by dumping a

pile of old newspapers, stacks of mail and other papers onto the floor. "Just a bunch of bills I can't pay," she said, kicking the pile aside.

Cole watched the pile of papers cascade into the pile of linoleum. "Uh, having some problems?"

Tray grabbed a coffeepot from the stove and held it up. "Want some?"

"Yes. Thanks."

As she poured the coffee, a long ash fell from her cigarette onto the floor. "My aunt was murdered, okay? Her estate and assets are frozen. Can't pay any of the bills from the house. Don't have the money. Can't sell the house, either, until the estate's settled." Tray sat down, stirring some creamer into her coffee. "Been talkin' to my aunt's lawyers all mornin'. Told 'em, y'all better get me some help here, or I'm gonna drown in debt that ain't even mine."

"What'd they say?"

"The usual lawyerly bullshit. I'm tellin' ya, the red tape's gonna choke and kill me before they ever get off square one." The portable phone rang. Tray answered it. "Hello? Yeah? I told you I already sent that. And you should already have the death certificate. Okay? Yeah, call me if you need anything else. Bye." Tray clicked the phone dead and threw it in the corner on top of yesterday's newspapers. "One of the paralegals. They keep askin' me for shit I've already sent 'em, when I really need 'em to handle this money crisis!"

Cole shrugged. "These things take time. Must be very frustrating for you."

"That's not the word I'd use."

"I'm sure it isn't. I'm assuming, when everything

is straightened out, that the debts will be paid from the estate."

"Yeah. But in the meantime, tell the electric company that." Tray lit another cigarette and threw the match into an old coffee cup. She rubbed her shoulder and grimaced. "This weather's murder on my shoulder."

"How's the rehab?"

"Shit, they kicked me out. Not any more they can do for me, unless I opt for surgery. But never mind that," Tray said, leaning back and crossing her legs. "Let's not talk about it."

"Sorry you're having such a rough time of it right now."

"Honey, I got more problems that an old alley cat has fleas." Tray inhaled deeply. "And it all started when that woman hit me broadside six months ago. I've got medical bills I can't pay and a lawsuit pendin' on that accident. In the meantime, I'm stuck with a monthly disability check that don't begin to pay everythin'."

Cole was hesitant to comment, but since Tray was so forthcoming with information, she decided to say what was on her mind. "Seems like a doctor would have pretty good disability coverage."

Tray shook her head in disgust. "Yeah, you'd think so, wouldn't ya. But not when you're an independent contractor with a temporary status. You must know somethin' about that."

"A little, yes."

"Worked at Grady Hospital in Atlanta. The second largest trauma center in the country. Unfortunately, I wasn't an employee of the hospital — and I wasn't makin' a million dollars like everyone thinks doctors make. Also didn't have any disability insurance of my own."

"Then what kind of disability are you on?"

"Government. Exactly six hundred and forty dollars a month."

Cole flinched in disbelief. "Oh my God. How do they expect you to live on that?"

"You tell me, babe."

"Geez, no wonder you're having problems."

"The hell with all that," Tray said, flipping ashes into the coffee cup. "You're here and I can gaze into your beautiful blue eyes. That's all that matters."

"Stop it."

"No, I mean it. You're so pretty. Didn't anyone ever tell you that?"

"Only you. If anyone did before, I paid no attention."

"You should've. Love lookin' at your eyes. So incredibly blue."

"Uh, I guess I should tell you. They're green."

Tray leaned forward and squinted. "Are not."

"Are too."

"No way, babe."

"Listen, it says 'green' on my birth certificate."

"I don't give a rat's ass what your birth certificate says. They're as blue as the sky, babe."

Cole shrugged and rested her head in her hands. "Whatever makes your Southern heart happy. Blue it is."

"You make my Southern heart happy." Tray grinned. "Never know, maybe someday soon the North will finally surrender to the South."

"Oh, really?" Cole asked, feigning shock.

"Nothin' like rewritin' the history books. Might even turn out to be fun."

"You never know," Cole commented wryly. She sipped her coffee, trying to analyze her inexplicable attraction to this woman, an attraction that seemed grounded in the sheer fascination of what Tray's life had already been. A poor Kentucky girl who had worked in the coal mines, to big-city hospital doctor saving lives in trauma rooms. Then the tragic accident, after which she'd been robbed of the profession she worked so long to achieve. Once again, she was penniless and fighting an uphill battle. It all seemed surreal to Cole. There was so much more she wanted to learn about Tray. Right now, what mattered most was that Cole mattered to Tray. Tray didn't seem confused about her feelings or her attraction to Cole. Her feelings were raw, exposed and very real. There was no need to overanalyze or scrutinize every single word that was or wasn't said. For that, Cole was grateful.

Cole slowly turned her key until the deadbolt clicked. It was after one in the morning. She and Tray had talked all day, gone for a long walk, and watched movies on television. Cole enjoyed the day. Tray had showered her with attention and compliments. She had to admit that it was nice being the center of attention again. It certainly had been a boost to her self-esteem.

Flipping on the kitchen light, Cole opened the

refrigerator. She was hungry and in the mood for a snack before bed. Staring into the refrigerator, she waited for something to catch her eye.

"Anything interesting going on in there?"

Cole jumped. It was Jan, clutching her robe with one hand while tugging her slippers on with the other. For a brief moment, Cole stared at the soft curves of cleavage made visible by Jan's robe. "Damn, you scared the hell out of me. Thought you were asleep."

"I was trying to sleep, Cole. But I was too worried about you. Where the hell have you been?"

Closing the refrigerator door, Cole grabbed a box of Ritz Bitz crackers from the cabinet above the built-in microwave. "Out. At a friend's house."

"What friend?"

Although it puzzled her, Cole sensed trouble. She popped a cracker into her mouth, wondering why on earth Jan cared who she was spending time with. "Tray Roberts," she mumbled while chewing. "Met her a couple weeks ago. Her aunt was murdered and I was beeped to the scene by the paper. That's when I ran into her."

Jan pursed her lips and raised her eyebrows. "Let me get this straight. A couple of weeks ago you met a woman at a murder scene — and tonight you stayed out with her until after one o'clock in the morning?"

Cole was still staring at the robe. It was short, stopping at mid-thigh, revealing enough skin to send a shiver of passion along Cole's spine. "Well, we were at her house." She shook the box and dug for another cracker, avoiding eye contact. "I mean, her aunt's house."

"Her dead aunt's house."

"Uh, yes. Dead aunt."

"Doing what?"

"Had the afternoon off. Stopped by to check on her. See how she was, you know, after the murder and all. We talked. Watched a movie on TV. No big deal."

"I was worried. Did it ever occur to you to call and let me know where you were?"

"Not really. No." Cole looked into the Ritz Bitz box. It was almost empty and the crackers were a little on the stale side.

"That's really cold."

"Well, I didn't know if you'd be here or not. You were working today, plus then you're usually out with friends." Cole threw the box of crackers into the garbage. "I never know when you're going to be around. Why should it be any different with me?"

"I always let you know where I am."

"Look, I'm sorry I didn't report in. But quite frankly, I was having fun. Something I haven't had in a long time."

Jan started tapping her foot, but with the slipper on it didn't have the same effect. "What's that supposed to mean?"

"You don't have any time for me. You've made that clear. You're on this I-need-to-find-myself kick. So, I try to stay out of your way. It's not the way I wanted it. So I think it's a little too late now for double standards."

A thin, caustic smile crossed Jan's face. "Why, Cole, that's the most emotion you've shown in months. Maybe you should get angry more often. Or visit a new friend's house more often."

Cole crossed her arms. She was hurt. "Go ahead. Slam me."

"I wasn't slamming you. That's always been one of

your problems. No communication. I never know what you're thinking. Whether you're angry, sad, happy, content."

"I was happy before all this. You made me happy."

"This is pointless. Go to bed."

Cole watched Jan leave. Her heart was pounding, the blood rushing in her ears. She was hurt and angry — and still her arms ached to hold Jan. But she knew that wasn't possible. Tonight she'd be staring at the ceiling in the den again, feeling guilty about her desire for Tray, a new set of emotions complicating everything else. She was suddenly aware of the dripping faucet at the kitchen sink. She'd really meant to fix that. Maybe this weekend.

For two weeks, Cole ignored Tray's phone calls at work. Uncertainty about her feelings for Tray, mixed with the hurt she felt over Jan, forced Cole into a state of confusion. The confusion finally lifted when loneliness and her desire to see Tray was all she could think about. Cole stopped by Tray's house for a visit and they went for a walk. The stinging wetness of a February snow blew against their faces. Saturday traffic was light and it was relatively quiet as they dodged the icy patches along the sidewalk. Shoulders touching, they walked hunched together against the cold air.

"I'm glad you stopped by, Cole." Tray smiled and threw her hair back over her shoulder. "Was kinda surprised you did."

"Why?"

"When you didn't return my calls, I figured you

were still hung up on Jan. Maybe you'd think of me as a threat instead of as a friend."

"Not at all. Never would have thought that. Anyway, it seems like Jan and I will always be past history."

"I'm sorry." Tray paused and put her arm around Cole's waist. "Sort of."

Cole laughed. "At least you're honest about your feelings."

Tray stopped and turned, looking directly at her. "To me, honesty and trust are everything, babe. If you don't have that in a relationship or friendship, you don't have anything."

"I agree."

"So many times in my life I've run into dishonest people or friends who break your trust and don't give a damn about doin' it. Guess that's why I'm really sensitive when it comes to honesty in relationships. There's just no sayin' how important that is."

"You're right. I don't think you can ever overstate the importance of being honest and truthful to the people you care about."

They started walking again. Cole hugged herself to block the cold. "Jan says I don't communicate well. Maybe it's true. But that doesn't mean I don't care. And it doesn't have anything to do with being honest or dishonest about my feelings."

"I think you communicate just fine."

"Do you?"

"Yeah. I like our talks. Could talk to you for hours, babe." Tray grinned. "But you let me talk far too much."

"It's fun to hear you talk." Cole stared at the pavement. "I may not be much of a conversationalist, but that doesn't mean I don't communicate. Sometimes not saying anything is saying enough."

"Well, I ain't never operated on that theory, honey, but I don't really disagree." Tray pointed to a small café on the next corner. "Coffee? We can sit and have a nice, long talk. Besides, I'm gettin' mighty cold out here," she said, pulling her jacket collar up. "It's colder than owl shit today."

"Okay, that's an expression I've never heard! Kentucky?"

"Honey, you can never take the Kentucky outta the girl."

"Guess not. Something to drink sounds good. Hot chocolate for me. Can't drink coffee in the middle of the day."

Tray grabbed a hold of Cole's arm, and steered her toward the café. "Baby, I can drink coffee any time of the day or night. It's the fuel that keeps me goin'."

"I've really missed you, Tray."

"I've missed you, too. You mustn't stay away this long again."

"I don't plan on it."

After the café, coffee and hot chocolate, after sliding back up the street over ice patches and snow, Cole stared at the ceiling. But it wasn't the ceiling in the den that had haunted her for months. It was the ceiling in Tray's bedroom, streaked with the last rays of afternoon sun. Suddenly, the ceiling became Tray's eyes, deep bronze like the streaks of light above them.

It was more than unsettling for Cole to be kissing

someone else. A part of her wanted to scream, "Stop!" But the part of her that hurt gave way.

"Don't be nervous, babe," Tray said, kissing her neck.

"I'm not," she lied.

Tray ran her fingers through Cole's hair. "Love your hair. Such beautiful curls and waves." Tray kissed her again. "So pretty," she whispered.

Cole closed her eyes to the kisses. She let feelings of anxious passion carry her into the moment and away from any doubt.

Tray blew out a candle. The shadows fell gray in the dusk, but Cole could still see the eyes that took her in. Tray wrapped Cole in her arms, the kisses more urgent, the grip of fingers into Cole's flesh pulling them closer together until Cole could feel Tray's body warm against her own.

Cole's lips trembled against Tray's until the long, deep kisses made her forget her nervousness. There was a hunger in their kisses, a longing for intimate contact that came not so much from affection as from loneliness.

There were tender kisses at Cole's neck and shoulders. Hungrier kisses at Cole's breasts where her nipples were drawn in between Tray's teeth and teased until they were hard and sensitive. Cole bit her bottom lip to keep from crying out. Because the name she thought of was not Tray's. It seemed so strange to be making love with someone else.

Tray ran her fingers between Cole's thighs. Cole could feel her own wetness as Tray entered her, stroking her slowly at first, then harder as Cole's breaths came in short gasps. The mechanics of it were right, Cole thought. A lesson in anatomy from a doctor? She was going to come hard in Tray's arms. It amazed her and surprised her. She thought it must happen all the time. One-night stands without passion, without love. Arousal for arousal's sake. But at least she cared for Tray. And with the aftermath of their lovemaking came an unusual sense of satisfaction. She found herself staring not at an empty ceiling, but at the bare skin of the arms that held and caressed her lovingly. In that there was satisfaction and temporary contentment.

The phone call from her brother had surprised her. It was an invitation to visit California for Easter. Cole didn't hesitate to accept, booking a flight immediately, excited for the opportunity to get away and visit with her niece, Amy.

Cole's sister-in-law intoned an Easter prayer. While Ruth prayed over the ham, Amy poked Cole under the table and giggled. Cole poked Amy back, secretly enjoying the irreverence of their actions. Her brother, Tony, and his wife, Ruth, were extremely religious. This was completely fine with Cole. She admired the strong commitment they demonstrated to their church and their beliefs. However, from time to time, she found herself subjected to Ruth's quiet indignation over her lifestyle. No words were ever expressly said, but Cole could read the signs. She knew, without verbal confirmation, exactly how Ruth felt about her. Due to this fact, visits to California to see her brother and niece were infrequent. But right now Cole was willing to endure Ruth's silent hostility just for the joy of seeing her brother and Amy again.

"Aunt Cole, look what happened," her four-year-old niece said, showing her a bandaged index finger.

"Oh, my. What in the world did you do to yourself?"

"It got caught."

"Caught? Where?"

"In my door."

Tony laughed as he carved the ham. "She's just learned the hard way that when you close a door, you have to remove your fingers first to get it to shut."

"I know that, Daddy. I forgot."

"Well, here, let me have a look." Cole examined the bandage and then kissed the tip of her niece's finger. "There. Now it will heal much faster."

Amy flashed a coy smile. "Thank you."

"You're welcome."

"Will you go for a walk with me after dinner?"

Ruth passed the platter of Easter ham to Cole. "She likes to go for walks to the park after supper," she said, stiffly. "It's right down the street."

"Oh, I'll be happy to take her." Cole took a slice of ham and laid it on her plate. She cut part of it into much smaller pieces and transferred them to Amy's plate. "Do you like ham?"

"Yes I do."

"She's beginning to eat more," Ruth said. "They go through these difficult eating phases when they're one, two, three. But I guess not having any children you wouldn't know about that."

Cole ignored the dig. She had vowed to be polite and upbeat at all times during the trip. "Oh, I know a little something about children. I do some volunteer work at a local hospital in Chicago. Put on puppet shows for the kids who are receiving dialysis and other treatments. They're all ages."

"I think that's great," Tony said. "How'd you get involved in that?"

"Saw an ad in the *Tribune* that the hospital needed volunteers."

"Aunt Cole, what's di-a-nol-sis?" Amy asked haltingly.

"Dialysis. When you're sick, it makes you feel better."

"Can you do a puppet show for me? I'm not sick."

"Of course I can. And you don't have to be sick. But you do have to eat some more dinner. You'll need the energy to go to the park."

Cole held Amy's hand as they crossed the street at the end of the block. The small park included a swing set, jungle gym, sandpit, seesaws and benches. It was a quaint neighborhood — a suburb of Los Angeles — with southwestern style homes made of stucco and cement.

"Mommy pushes me on the swings," Amy announced, running toward the empty swing set.

"Well, good. I can push you, too."

"Oh, boy!"

Amy sat on a swing, legs straight out, and Cole began to push her.

"Not too high!"

"Okay. You tell me when it gets too high."

"Aunt Cole, why do you live so far away?"

"Because that's where I work, sweetie. In Chicago."

"Oh."

"Maybe someday you can come to Chicago and visit me."

"Can I?"

"If your parents say it's okay."

"Do you have parks in Chicago?"

"We have great big parks in Chicago."

"Bigger than this one?"

"Much bigger. With fountains and lakes and ducks."

"Ducks!"

"Ducks."

"When we go back home can we ask if I can visit you?"

"Of course we can." Cole kept pushing the swing gently, keeping it at a steady height. As she watched her niece's long blond hair flying in the breeze, she knew that the possibility of her brother, his wife and Amy making a trip to Chicago was highly unlikely. But maybe someday, she thought, when Amy was old enough, she would choose to visit on her own.

"Aunt Cole!"

"What? Is this too high?"

"No. I love you."

"I love you, too."

Cole snatched the Saturday paper out of the vending machine. As she walked back down the street to Tray's house, she noticed that the late-April sun was slowly coaxing the tulip bulbs out of the earth. In a couple of weeks they would be blooming in red, yellow, purple and hybrid colors.

"Anything interestin' in the news?" Tray asked, perched on the sofa.

Cole dropped the paper on Tray's lap. "Not much." The phone rang. Tray continued to peruse the newspaper and made no move to answer it. "Want me to get that?"

"Yeah. You mind?"

"Not at all." Cole answered the portable phone in the kitchen. "Who's calling, please? Just a minute." Cole muffled the phone. "Tray, it's for you. Nation's Credit, or something like that."

"Oh, well tell 'em I'm not home."

"Okay. Excuse me, I'm sorry. She's out right now. Can I take a message? Jill Simons. Yes, give me the number." Cole scribbled down the phone number and hung up. "Some creditor, Tray. I wrote down the number for you."

"Yeah, fine."

"That was the fifth call this week — at least the ones I answered since I got back from my trip."

"Yeah, well creditors tend to call when you owe 'em money."

"Aren't you the least little bit concerned about these calls?"

"No. I just ignore 'em."

"Do you think that's wise?"

"What would you like me to do? Unless money starts growin' on trees, there ain't much I can do."

The phone calls from the creditors bothered Cole. She was sure Tray was going to be hauled off at any moment by the police because of indebtedness — all caused by a car accident and a murder that weren't her fault. "Well, maybe I can help pay a few bills for you, until you get things settled with the lawyers."

"No. I couldn't let you do that. Thanks anyway."

"Why not? What's the difference? You can pay me back. Think of it as a small loan. At least it will get some of these creditors off your back."

"I'll think about it. Let's forget it for now. Want to go see a movie?"

"Sure. Sounds like fun."

Tray tossed the paper aside and got up. She kissed Cole on the forehead. "Listen to me. There's a word I think about an awful lot. It's *pride*. I ain't got much of it left, so please don't ask me to give up anymore. Not just yet."

Cole felt terrible. "I'm so sorry. I care about you and I know you're in trouble."

"And I care about you, too. Let's just leave it there for now. When the time comes to really start worryin', I'll let you know."

Chapter Six

Cole leaned against the wall, arms crossed, gazing out Jan's bedroom window. It was Monday, the first day of May. The sun was warm, streaming across the front yard through the glass and onto her face. The snow had finally melted and the city was thawing from the cold, empty streets of winter into the bustling activity of spring. Kids, just out of school for the day, were playing ball in an empty lot. A woman was walking her little white poodle and a lawn service was mowing the grass across the street.

Suddenly, Cole snapped out of her sun-induced daze and turned from the window to snatch a pair of jeans out of the bottom dresser drawer. Nervously, she checked her watch. It was after three o'clock and she wanted to be out of the house before Jan came home from work. Their encounters had been few over the past two months. They had seen each other at the hospital, to pay bills and to plan for some repairs to the house. The unplanned encounters were more painful. Cole could barely get through them without feeling physically sick.

Truthfully, except to use her darkroom, Cole hadn't been inside the house for long stretches of time. She had access to the darkroom through a locked basement door. During all their years together, Jan had never bothered her while she was working in the darkroom. And that had not changed. Cole had simply slipped in and out of the basement each day, completing her work and leaving immediately.

While unzipping her sports bag, Cole thought she heard the front door open. She winced. Jan was home early. Today was going to be one of those days.

Cole listened to the footsteps along the hallway. Quickly, she shoved the rest of her clothes into the sports bag, zipped it up and hoisted it over her shoulder to signal she was in a hurry. That she couldn't stay and argue, that today there would be no drawn-out anxious scene.

"Well, well. Cole Evans. What brings you to our humble home? Run out of clothing?"

Slowly, Cole turned. When she saw Jan, her stomach burned, sending a painful sensation all the way up her chest. There were circles under Jan's eyes and she looked at least five pounds thinner. "Please, Jan. Let's not fight. I can't stand it anymore. Besides, I really have to get going."

"Why aren't you at work?"

"I've got the day off."

"How nice."

"I miss you." Cole looked away from Jan and back to the window. In just that few minutes, the sun had slipped behind storm clouds. How appropriate. "Unfortunately, every time I see you we're at each other's throats."

"How do you expect me to feel?" Jan asked in a strained voice, standing squarely in the doorway. "I ask for a little space to sort out my feelings, and what do you do? Go off merrily and find yourself a new girlfriend. How much do you think that hurts?"

Cole shrugged helplessly and fought back tears. "I didn't mean for it to happen this way. But I was lonely. Honestly, the way things were going, I didn't know if you'd ever want me back."

"You never gave me a chance to decide what I wanted."

Through the tears, Cole fought to keep her composure. She spun around and asked, "How many months did you need? Eight? Ten? A whole year? How long was I supposed to wait to find out if I was good enough for you?"

"I don't know. But I thought you'd have enough respect to give the two of us a chance again. To come to me and talk if you had these feelings for Tray. I think I deserved that much instead of finding out when you didn't come home for two months."

"I'm sorry." Cole stepped toward the door. "I didn't

mean to hurt you. I've been confused, Jan. And Tray made me feel wanted again. Like I mattered. I missed that and I never wanted it from anybody else but you."

"Well, I'm sure you're getting plenty of attention now."

"Like I said before, I do miss you very much."

"Then come home."

"I can't. I'm the one who needs some time now. To see what *I* want."

Jan flashed a bitter smile. "Touché. I guess there's not much I can say to that."

"Guess not."

"We have to talk finances at some point. Had to have the roof fixed. Leaked during that heavy rain last week. I have the bill."

"Oh, okay. Leave it on the kitchen table. I'll look at it tomorrow. I'll be using the darkroom."

"Fine. I'll leave it for you. The electric and gas bills are due, too."

"I'll bring my checkbook and write you one check for everything."

"Thanks. Do you love this woman?"

"I care about her." Cole looked down at the floor. "*Love* may not be the right word."

"Well, you've told me enough about Tray to know that she certainly needs someone in her life right now," Jan said, stepping into the hallway. "I can't blame her for choosing you to provide that support. I'm sure you've been a big help to her, Cole."

"I've tried. We'll talk again soon."

* * * * *

Lugging the sports bag over her shoulder, Cole trudged up Tray's front steps. Tray met her at the door. "Hey, babe. Been waitin' for you." Tray's arms wrapped themselves around her. The hug was strong and reassuring. "Come with me. Got a surprise for you."

Cole smiled. "A surprise? You're always full of surprises."

"In more ways than one," Tray agreed with a smile.

Tray led Cole by the hand into the bathroom. The tub was filled with steaming water, candles were lit and a large, frozen strawberry daiquiri topped with whipped cream was sitting on the edge of the tub.

"Wanted to pamper you. Know you've been out of sorts lately," Tray said in a comforting tone. "Relax in the tub and enjoy. I'll be in the next room waitin' for you."

Cole soaked and basked in the hot water trying not to think about her confrontation with Jan. Then she wrapped herself in a towel and went into Tray's bedroom. Maybe this would be a way to forget.

The room was glowing with candles, the soft light dancing between the shadows. Red satin sheets were on the bed. Strawberries covered with powdered sugar were in a bowl on the bedside table. A bottle of wine rested in an ice bucket.

Tray handed Cole a glass of white zinfandel. "Hey, beautiful."

"Hey."

Tray leaned forward and pressed her mouth hard against Cole's — her tongue filling Cole's mouth with passion. At the same time, her hands slowly removed the towel from Cole's shoulders, her strong fingers running along Cole's warm skin. With a heavy sigh, Tray lowered herself across Cole's body, her tongue running wild along Cole's neck and shoulders, her breath hot, her kisses rough.

Feeling Tray's teeth sink into the hard skin at her breast, Cole arched her back, forcing herself deeper into Tray's grasp. In a slow, agonizing tempo, Tray traveled every crevice of Cole's body with her mouth until her tongue entered her, fucked her with its smooth, hot flesh. Then Tray's fingers slid inside and with hard, thundering strokes, Cole shuddered as she came.   *

The candles danced and fluttered, matching the rhythm of Cole's heart.

Cole woke up with a start. She looked around the candlelit room and realized that she had fallen asleep. The wine, the orgasms, the whispered conversation had faded with a peaceful slumber. Tray was gone.

Cole threw her legs over the side of the bed, grabbed her robe and slipped it on. At the end of the hall, she made a right into the den and found Tray hovered over the computer. The computer had belonged to her aunt, who used it to track stocks and commodities. According to what Tray had told Cole, her aunt, Gloria Ramsey, was twice divorced and once widowed. The money her husbands had given to her or left her had once been a handsome sum. But over the years, through a series of unwise investments and too many trips to the horse-betting tracks, the funds were squandered away. The only asset Mrs. Ramsey had managed to hang onto was the house, which was in great need of repair.

Cole put her hands on Tray's shoulders and bent down to kiss her neck.

"Hey, babe. Sleep okay?"

"Yes, thanks. Gave you a chance to get some work done, I see."

"I've been lookin' into some things on the Internet, tryin' to think of a way to make some money. Whoever had the idea to rob my aunt sure as hell came to the wrong address," Tray said sarcastically. "If she'd had ten bucks in her purse, it woulda been a miracle."

Cole looked over Tray's shoulder. "Have you thought of what to do about all the bills?"

"Actually, that's what I'm workin' on right now." Tray bookmarked the Web site she had found. "I think I already told you that when I was a doctor I had a hobby that I worked at in my spare time." Tray talked through the smoke she had just inhaled. "Not that I had much spare time. But I needed somethin' to do — just for fun and relaxation."

"Yes, you said you did flower arranging."

"That's right. Just like the one on the coffee table in the living room."

"The one you made as a birthday present for your aunt. Very classy."

"Thanks, babe. Now, since I can't practice medicine anymore, I'm thinkin' of startin' my own business at it." Tray's eyes beamed with excitement. "Thought I could open my own shop or work out of the house here. Maybe even design a Web site to do some mail order business."

"Sounds like a great idea."

Tray's shoulders slumped forward and her face drooped like a basset hound's. "Yeah, it would be if I weren't bogged down in all this debt my aunt left behind. I need some capital to start the business. Until my aunt's estate is free and I can sell the house, or until my accident suit is settled, I'm really strapped for cash."

Cole patted Tray's shoulder. "The age-old problem. Need money to make money."

"Yep, that's the way it works."

"What are you going to do?"

"Well, I was sorta hopin' you could help me out, babe." Tray's eyes darted back and forth. "Believe me, I wouldn't ask if I thought I could get any kinda loan from a bank. But right now, with all this mess, it just ain't gonna happen."

"How much do you need?"

"Damn, this is downright embarrassin'. Havin' to ask your girlfriend for a loan. If I had a speck of pride left before, sure as hell don't now."

Putting her arms around Tray's shoulders, Cole said, "Don't be so hard on yourself. Tell me how much you need."

"Well, fifteen thousand should at least get me started. But I absolutely insist on doin' the whole thing legal-like. I'll get my aunt's lawyers to draw up some loan papers. As soon as my accident claim or my aunt's estate gets settled, I promise to pay you back with interest."

Cole sat down. It was a lot of money. But she felt terrible for Tray and her current circumstances. None of it was her fault. A series of unfortunate tragedies had left her in a real financial bind. "I don't object to the loan at all, Tray. And don't worry about the legal stuff. We'll work it out. First, I'll have to see how much I can borrow. Maybe I can get a credit union loan through the *Trib*. When do you need the money?"

"Babe, as soon as you can throw me a life raft is as soon as I'll get my ass outta deep water." Tray laughed nervously and clutched Cole's hand. "Appreciate your lookin' into this for me. Even if you can't help, knowin' that you'd try means a lot to me."

"Hey, it's okay. Really."

Tears welled in Tray's eyes. "Never thought things would get this low. Work all your life and think you've finally made a way for yourself. Then life knocks you down and you wonder if you'll ever get up again."

"You'll get up again. And you'll be better than ever."

"Thanks for the vote of confidence."

"A strong vote of confidence. By the way, I want you to meet Jackson. I'm having dinner with him tomorrow night. And David, his boyfriend. Can you make it?"

"I've got a few appointments, but I'll try."

"Good. It'll be fun. I know you'll love the guys."

"Lookin' forward to it."

The following evening, when Cole arrived at the restaurant she found Jackson alone, hurling darts at an electronic dartboard trying to impress himself, if no one else. A few minutes later, Cole was also lobbing darts. The multicolored plastic board beeped loudly and flashed numbers whenever a dart landed. Unfortunately, her darts seemed to find a home on the floor rather than on the board.

"No, no. You've got to lean into the shot like this." Jackson threw the dart and it landed in the green circle right outside the red bull's-eye.

Cole grinned. "Uh, yes. Okay. Let me give it a try." Cole grasped the dart between her thumb and forefingers. She squinted and aimed, leaning into the shot as instructed. The dart bounced off the edge of the board and hit the floor.

Jackson doubled over with laughter. "Great shot, Cole."

"Hey, I only did what you told me."

"Obviously, you need some more practice."

"Okay. Next time we play, it'll be with a wager." She picked up the dart and stuck it into the board. The board beeped defiantly. "C'mon, I'll buy you another beer."

"That's the way it should be. Loser always buys."

"I thought the winner always buys."

"That depends on whether I've won or lost."

"Ahhh, I see how it works." Cole leaned against Jackson's shoulder. He put his arm around her and they walked over to the bar.

"So, tell me more about Tray. What's going on with you two? Haven't gotten a word out of you recently."

"That's painful for you, I'm sure. But you'll meet her tonight, so your curiosity will be satisfied. At least for a little while."

"I pride myself in knowing all your deep, dark secrets."

"Well, I'm afraid I don't have any earth-shattering

revelations about Tray. I'm just taking things slowly. She's a really neat person, but she's got a lot of problems. Mostly financial. In fact, she's asked me to help her."

"Help her with her finances?"

"She wants me to lend her some money."

"And . . ."

"I want to help her. It's a lot of money, but she's in a real bind."

"How much does she need, if you don't mind my asking?"

"No. It's okay. Fifteen thousand dollars."

Jackson stopped drinking mid-sip and lowered his beer glass. He stared at Cole, his eyes searching hers.

"I know. It's a lot of money. But she's going to pay me back."

"Hell, yes, it's a lot of money. When's she going to pay you back?"

"As soon as she sells her aunt's house. Or as soon as she gets a settlement from the car accident she was in. Shouldn't be long from what she says. Her lawyers are working hard to resolve the mess."

"Sounds reasonable," Jackson said, leaning his elbow on the bar. "But you should have her sign a paper or something." Jackson put his hand on her shoulder. "I mean, you trust her and I understand that. Or you wouldn't be lending her the money. Still, you should have some record of it."

Cole nodded in agreement. "Tray's already offered to have her lawyers draw up loan papers. So that's not an issue."

"You in love with her?"

She quickly looked away. "Uh, gosh. It's too early to say, I think. I mean, I care about her, you know?"

"Sure."

"There's something about her that's intriguing. Can't quite put my finger on it. Plus, to be honest, I've been kinda lonely since Jan —"

"Went on her 'vision quest'? I know you have. And, whatever happens, I'm glad you have someone who at least fills some need."

Cole glanced at her watch. "Speaking of love, when's this handsome man of yours going to get here?"

Jackson craned his neck to glance outside. "Actually, just saw his car pull up out front. Now he's giving his keys to the valet."

"Cool. Can't wait to see him again."

"He really likes you. Thinks you're a doll."

"Ha! Obviously, he doesn't know me that well."

"You are a doll."

"Listen, I think David's an absolute gem. But I knew if you loved him that I was going to love him, too."

A few minutes later, a tall muscular man walked into the restaurant and strolled toward the bar. He had a closely shaven beard, dark hair with blond highlights and a Clark Gable smile.

"Hey, look at you two! Already a beer ahead of me. Sorry I'm late." David put his arm around Cole's shoulder and kissed her on the cheek. "How've you been, sweetie?"

"Good. You?"

David loosened his tie and removed his suit jacket, hanging it over the back of the barstool. "Busy day." He turned to Jackson and hugged him tightly. "Missed you, baby."

"Missed you, too. These workdays seem much

longer than they used to when I didn't have you in my life," Jackson said. "Hungry?"

"Yeah, but I'll have a beer first." David sat down on the barstool between them. "What a beautiful day. Spring is finally here, thank God."

Cole looked outside. The sun was setting and the sky was on fire. "I love my job when the weather's nice. Working outside has its benefits, especially on days like this."

"That's a great perk, for sure," David agreed. "I'm afraid I don't have that luxury anymore. Used to when I was part of the sales team. Now that I manage the team, I mostly attend meetings and track regional sales. Just got back from a business meeting in Lisle. The traffic was pretty bad. That's why I'm late."

Jackson laughed. "The traffic was bad 'cause everyone left work early to enjoy what they could of this warm weather."

"By the way, David, I just read an article about your company," Cole interrupted. "They're considered one of the top ten companies to work for in the country according to *Fortune* magazine."

David poured his beer into a frosted mug. "Yeah, I saw that article, too. It was posted on the company intranet. Quite frankly, I have to agree. It's really an excellent outfit to work for."

"He's got fifteen people working under him," Jackson said. "They got top sales for the country last year."

Cole smiled and nodded. "Congratulations."

"And now I've met Jackson," David said, putting

his arm around Jackson's shoulder. "How much better could life be?"

"I don't think it gets any better than that. Say, do you play darts?" Cole asked.

David chuckled. His deep-set eyes met hers. "I can hold my own." David nodded his head toward Jackson. "He been hustling you?"

"Yes, he has. Pretended to help me and I ended up playing even worse than before."

"Hmmm, imagine that. But maybe we can do something about it," David said thoughtfully, rubbing his chin. He turned toward Jackson. "What do you say there, champ? Or should I say, chump? Man enough to take us both on?"

"I'll take both of you on, no problem. Even spot you some points," Jackson challenged, getting up from his chair.

"Oh, no. That won't be necessary will it, Cole?"

"You kidding? We don't need any points. We'll whip his butt on sheer talent alone."

"Oh, brother," Jackson said. "This is going to be way too much fun."

David got up and took Cole's hand. He whispered in her ear, "That's the way to intimidate him, partner. Ready?"

Cole smiled. "Ready."

"Loser buys dinner," David said, giving Cole a reassuring look.

Jackson picked up the darts and reset the scoreboard. "Then I'll be eating well tonight."

A half hour later, Cole ordered the mixed seafood platter and David chose a huge sirloin.

"What are you having, Jackson?" Cole asked.

"A small dinner salad," Jackson grumbled. "A very small dinner salad."

Cole and David laughed until tears stung their eyes.

David patted Jackson on the shoulder. "We'll make sure they throw a couple of croutons on it."

"Gosh, thanks." Jackson slapped the menu on the table. "Hustled by my best friend and lover. Who'd ever believe it?"

"Hey y'all."

"Tray!" Cole said. "We were getting worried."

Both Jackson and David stood up. David took Tray's overcoat and draped it over her chair.

"Thanks," Tray said. "Thought it was gonna rain."

"You're welcome. I'm David Tanner."

"Nice meetin' you, David."

Jackson leaned over and shook Tray's hand. "Jackson Ward. Pleasure to meet you."

"Nice meetin' you, too. Sorry I'm late. Got tied up. Business." Tray sat down, dropping her briefcase next to her. She was dressed in a tan suit jacket, matching slacks and a silk blouse. "I'm glad y'all went ahead and ordered. Not very hungry anyway."

"Well, at least let's get you a drink." David flagged down the waiter and ordered a beer for Tray.

Cole leaned over and kissed Tray on the cheek. "So, what have you been up to today?"

"Aw, y'all don't wanna talk business now, do you?"

David laughed. "Hey, they had to listen to my sad tale about traffic and meetings running late. So feel free."

Tray picked up her briefcase. "Well, I've been workin' with a graphics artist to help me design a business card and marketing brochure for the new business I'm startin'. I've got some rough sketches. Maybe y'all can give me your opinions."

"We'd love to," Cole offered. "Besides, we have a professional right here at the table. Jackson manages the creative department for an ad agency."

Jackson smiled. "Be happy to look at the sketches, but Cole always over-inflates my expertise."

"The hell I do."

Tray took out the boards and held them up. There were two business card designs. "Well, what do y'all think?"

"I like this one," David said, indicating the card with the gray background and raised floral graphic in a deep mauve. "Not that I know anything, mind you."

"Actually, I like that one, too." Jackson pointed to the floral illustration. "This has nice lines and the design is very hip and nineties. Very contemporary, if that's what you're trying to communicate."

"That's it exactly," Tray agreed.

"You should see her floral arrangements," Cole said. "There's one at her aunt's house that's absolutely stunning."

Jackson looked at the second board with the brochure layout and design. "This is good, too. But it's a bit heavy on copy. I think another illustration on the middle panel will break it up for you. Give it a cleaner look."

Tray nodded. "Thanks. Really appreciate your help."

"No problem," Jackson said. "If you need anymore help, here's my business card. Just give me a call."

They all sat for a while, had another drink and chatted. Cole was pleased that Tray had finally met some of her friends. It was a comfortable gathering — with lots of laughter and conversation. In the past months, as she spent more and more time with her support group, Jan had withdrawn from Cole's friends. Cole had missed that much-needed camaraderie and feeling of family.

Chapter Seven

Parking the car around the corner from Tray's house, Cole felt exhausted. During the past week, work had been hell. She had logged at least twelve hours of overtime — most of it cooped up in the bowels of her darkroom with the sound of Jan's footsteps passing overhead. It had been unnerving. She was thankful it was Friday and that she had the weekend free.

Despite the busy week, Cole was finally able to make it into the credit union to pick up the loan money for Tray. She'd carried the check folded up in her wallet for three days. Things had been so crazy at work, she'd almost forgotten about it.

When Cole handed the check to Tray, she proceeded to collapse in a heap on the sofa. She burst into uncharacteristic tears. Cole wasn't sure what to say or do. She squeezed Tray's shoulder and looked up at the ceiling, thinking the reaction was a bit melodramatic. Finally she asked, "Hey, you okay?"

"Yeah, babe. I'm fine."

"Uh, well, you're kind of hysterical. So, I thought I should ask."

"Sorry. Don't usually get this upset. Just don't know what I'd do without you." Tray looked up, lips trembling, eyes still tearing. "Fact is, don't know how I made it this long without someone like you in my life."

Cole stumbled over her words. "It's okay. Really. Everything's going to be fine."

"Thanks to you."

Cole sat down on the sofa while Tray lit a cigarette. The large, black ashtray next to Tray was overflowing with ashes and cigarette butts. "Listen, you don't have to chain-smoke yourself to death. You know, for someone who used to be a doctor, you sure smoke a lot. I thought all doctors had given up the bad habit."

"Bullshit. They just do it in secret now."

"That surprises me. But if you say so."

"Besides, I ain't a doctor anymore."

"Well, now that you've got some funds, you can stop feeling sorry for yourself and start your new business. Then, your money worries will be over."

"I know. I know," Tray said, waving the cigarette

at her. "I'm just a little depressed. So much has happened in the last nine months."

"Listen to me. I can understand why you'd be overwhelmed. You've been through an awful lot. The accident, injuries, rehab, losing your career. Then, on top of all that, your aunt is horribly murdered."

"I'll be okay."

"Of course you will. We'll get through this together."

"Listen, my lawyers are still workin' on the loan papers. Man, these people are slower than slugs. Sorry, I don't have 'em yet." Tray handed the check back to Cole. "You keep this until the papers are ready."

Cole shook her head and waved the check away. "No, that's fine. You need the money now. Get your business cards and brochures printed. We'll worry about the papers later. Say, how did you make out with your appointment at Holiday Inn?"

Tray folded the check and put it in her back pocket. "Holiday Inn?"

"Yeah, you said you were working on a deal to decorate their lobbies."

Tray laughed. "Sorry, how could I forget? You see, I am losin' my mind."

"No, you're not. Like you said, a lot has happened."

Tray drew her knees up against her chest and curled into the corner of the sofa. "Yeah, I saw the guy yesterday. Showed him some photos of my work. Said he'd get back to me early next week."

"Well, if he doesn't, you should follow up. I'm not an expert on sales, but I know you've got to keep after them."

Tray reached across the end table and punched out her cigarette butt. "So, now that you've financed my business, you gonna tell me how to run it?" Tray laughed half-heartedly, but Cole heard the sarcasm in her voice. The tears and gratefulness had suddenly dried up. Now a different Tray stared at her.

"No, of course not. Was just trying to help. You're the expert, not me."

Tray's brown eyes flashed black. "Sorry, babe. I've had about all I can take right now."

Cole could see that and was greatly concerned. Tray's appearance was frightful. She was dressed in wrinkled clothes that looked like they had been slept in, and her features were drawn. There were heavy circles under her eyes. Her hair was stringy and hanging in her face. She looked like she'd gotten out of bed that morning, made it as far as the sofa — and that was it. "Hey, no problem. How about we go grab a bite to eat? My treat."

"I'll have to quick take a shower. Can't go out lookin' like this."

"I can amuse myself for a while. Take your time."

Tray got up from the sofa, leaned over and kissed Cole on top of the head. "Ya know, you didn't take me to raise. You've been payin' all the bills around here for the last month — and now you've loaned me money to start a business. I'm the one who should be treatin' you to dinner."

"You will. It won't be long now and you will."

"Glad someone has confidence in me."

"Have all the confidence in the world in you."

"My mom used to say that to run with the big

dogs, you gotta first get off the porch. Not so sure I'm ready."

"You're ready. Wait and see. You're going to be great."

Tray shuffled toward the staircase. "Thanks, I needed that," she called back. "I'm lucky to have you in my life. Don't think I don't know it."

Cole heard Tray take the steps slowly. Then the bathwater started to run. Grabbing the newspaper, Cole propped her feet up on the sofa. Someone actually needed her, she thought. It was a refreshing change from the past.

Suddenly, the weekend was a memory. Late Monday afternoon Cole found herself back at work, staring at a six-alarm fire racing through a downtown apartment complex. She had positioned herself across the street, just south of the police barricades. Deep in thought, she studied the scene carefully, trying to determine how to get the best angle. She wanted to stay out of the way of the firefighters doing their job. There were people still trapped inside the smoke-engulfed building. One older Hispanic woman was screaming in Spanish, hanging halfway out her upper-floor apartment window, the smoke billowing from behind her into the late-afternoon air.

"Hey, baby. We meet again, clandestinely."

"Kay! The absolute sunshine of my life."

"Humph. I doubt that."

Cole laughed and gripped Kay's hand, gently

pulling her from the crowd. "Listen, I'm going to try to get inside this building and head up to the rooftop," Cole said, nodding toward the office building behind them. "I know you're the competition, but wanna come along?"

"Competition, maybe. But we're also friends. Be nice to have an adventure together. Let's go."

The two women raced into the building and ran headlong into the building's security team. Flashing their press badges, they insisted on being allowed access to the rooftop due to the emergency across the street. Somewhat intimidated by the credentials of Chicago's two major newspapers, the guards reluctantly sent them up via the freight elevator. The large, if somewhat slower, elevator offered direct access to the roof. One of the security guards accompanied them.

"Now, you two ladies aren't going to do anything foolish to get me into trouble, are you?" he asked with a nervous smile.

"No," Kay said, while reloading her camera. "We really appreciate your cooperation."

"Sure," the guard said. "Shouldn't be much longer now."

The elevator ground to an abrupt halt. The large doors slid open and led to a short staircase to the roof. Once on the roof, Kay and Cole surveyed the scene across from them. They both set up their equipment and took some shots. Cole circled the expanse of the rooftop, still not happy with the angle. They were a little too low, she thought. A couple more stories and they'd have the ideal perspective. Then she eyed the heating and refrigeration equipment located at the center of the flat roof. If she could manage to scramble to the top of that surface, the extra height would allow her a downward perspective. With the proper lens she would be able to shoot the entire scene, including the pandemonium at street level.

Cole glanced at the guard who already looked worried. She doubted he would permit her to climb the large, metal structure.

"Ready to leave?" the guard asked gruffly. He stared at his watch, obviously anxious to get going.

"Yes, I'm ready. What about you, Kay?"

"Sure. Not much to shoot up here."

The three of them approached the rooftop exit. Stopping to adjust some of her equipment, Cole managed to get the guard to go through the door first. Kay stayed behind her. As soon as the guard disappeared through the door Cole slammed it, latching it shut with an outside sliding bolt. She could hear the guard screaming through the door and pounding on it with his fist.

"Cole, what the hell are you doing?" Kay asked with a sly grin.

"I'm going to get a better angle, that's what. I suppose you noticed our perspective was all wrong up here."

"Of course. That's why I only popped a couple."

Cole pointed to the heating and air conditioning equipment. "I'll need your help to get up there."

Kay eyed the large entanglement of metal. "You're crazy, Cole Evans. First of all, you'll break your lovely neck. Second, my job is not to help you get the best photo for the competition."

"You help get me up there and the photo will have both our names on it. Remember, I'm just a lowly freelancer."

Kay laughed, dropping her equipment bag to the ground. "I always knew there was a reason I liked you, Evans. Aside from the fact that I think you're pretty damned cute."

"Uh, thanks," Cole said, turning away, embarrassed by the compliment. "Now, give me a boost."

The large hunk of metal sat on a concrete platform, which created a ledge. Cole hopped up on the ledge, then held out her hand to Kay.

"All right, now that we're both situated, I'll give you a boost. Then I'll toss your equipment up." Kay hunched over and locked the fingers of her hands together. Cole inserted her foot and Kay gave her a leg up. In fact, Kay boosted her with such force that Cole cleared the next ledge and slammed into a wall of metal.

"Hey, you okay, Evans? Have you killed yourself yet?"

"No, damn it. Send up my pack."

"Here it comes."

The canvas equipment bag rose in the air just in front of Cole and she snatched it in midflight. It was a perfect toss. The last ledge to the top was lower, but nonetheless tricky. She'd have to scale it herself, heaving the equipment up first. She flung the canvas bag up and heard it land with a heavy clunk.

"Cole?" she heard Kay yell.

"I'm okay. It was the camera bag landing."

"Good. I thought it was your dead body hitting the roof. Was just about to come up and look for you."

"Gee, thanks."

"No problem."

Cole positioned her hands on top of the last ledge. It was about six feet high to her five foot seven. She pulled with all her might, digging her feet into the wall, trying to gain some leverage. But the wall was made out of steel and was slick with condensation. Finally, she gave up and shimmied her way to the other side where she found a vent. The vent made a perfect step and she was able to scoot over the top of the wall. Immediately, she located her camera bag and prepared her equipment. The light was still adequate and when she looked down to the scene below, she realized that her calculations were correct. The height she had gained by climbing up there gave her the ideal perspective she needed.

In quick succession, Cole fired off about ten shots. The top of the heating and air conditioning unit was slick, and twice she nearly lost her balance. Finally, when she was certain she had what she needed, she carefully made her way back to the rooftop. As she neared the last ledge, she threw her bag down to Kay, who then caught her in her arms as she slid down the final wall onto the concrete slab.

Kay held her there for a brief moment. Cole's legs were wobbly.

"You okay, sport?" Kay asked, still clutching Cole's waist.

"Uh, yes." Cole looked up and met the gaze of two very attractive hazel eyes. Kay was smiling. "Must be getting too old for this."

"I don't think so," Kay politely disagreed. "Personally, I enjoyed the entire adventure. We must work together more often."

Cole laughed and moved away to pick up her bag. "Yes, it was fun, Kay. Thanks."

"My pleasure."

Kay unbolted the rooftop door. The security guard

was still there, sitting on the top step. Instantly, he shot to his feet and looked at them both sternly.

"I guess it would be too much to ask what in the hell you ladies were doing up there?"

"You get the newspaper?" Cole asked.

The guard glared at her and didn't answer.

"Check out the front page in the local section of the *Tribune* tomorrow," Cole instructed. "Then you'll see. And when you're done checking out the *Tribune*, buy the *Sun-Times*."

"You should buy the *Sun-Times* first," Kay said with a wink. "Much better paper, though I mean no disrespect to my colleague."

The security guard sighed, turned and headed down the steps. "Get the hell onto the elevator, ladies. And if I don't personally toss both of you into the street by the seat of your pants you'll be lucky." The guard punched the button for the first floor. "Reporters," he mumbled. "Always trouble."

Kay gave Cole a sideways glance and a smile. "Want to grab a bite to eat? After all that excitement, I'm hungry."

"Great idea. You mind driving?"

"Not at all."

The restaurant was a small hole-in-the-wall establishment that served excellent Mexican food. Cole and Kay munched on chips and salsa while waiting for their entrees.

"So, what you been up to, Evans? How's Jan?"

"Uh, Jan's fine. Real good," Cole replied, stumbling over her words. She didn't feel like having that conversation today. "You with anybody right now?"

"Have you ever known me to be?" Kay asked, sarcastically. "You know I'm a loner, Cole."

Cole stared at the sea-colored eyes. They looked big enough to swallow her up, if she didn't dive into them first. "Yes, but you date. So you're not always alone."

"I date when I meet someone interesting. Needless to say, I don't date too often."

"You're something else."

"Listen, I adore the company of a woman for a night or two. Maybe even a week. After that, they get too damned needy. Everything changes. All the excitement goes out of it."

"You just haven't met the right person."

Kay leaned forward, her cheeks still ruddy from the cold. "Hey, I've got this perfect life scenario, okay?"

"What would that be?"

"It's like this, okay? I adore all my women friends. And I count you among them, just for the record."

"Uh, thanks, Kay. That's nice to know."

"So here's my fantasy. I rent a hotel suite. The best in the city. That's where I live. I invite one of my women friends over each night of the week, because I've got a special affinity for every one of them."

"And?"

"And we have a wonderful dinner, a glass of good wine, and we fuck each other's brains out all night long. In the morning, she leaves."

"The friend."

"Yes, exactly. Next night, it all starts again. With a different friend, of course."

"Of course."

"Whaddya think?"

"Sounds intriguing."

"You can have Saturday nights if you want. Only the best for you." Kay roared with laughter and squeezed Cole's arm. "We all have our fantasies. Nothing wrong with that."

"Not at all."

"What's yours?"

"Uh, gee. I don't know."

Kay wagged her finger at Cole. "No, no. Not fair. C'mon."

Cole wanted to tell Kay about the tall redheaded stranger she was sleeping with. But she couldn't. It was too soon to talk about Tray. So she thought of another redhead. A famous one. "Susan Hayward. She's my fantasy."

"Susan Hayward?"

"Uh-huh. Movie star. Absolutely gorgeous. Legitimate fantasy material."

"Yeah, except there's a slight problem with that fantasy, Cole. She's dead."

"No kidding."

"That's cheating, but I'll let you off the hook anyway."

"Gosh, thanks."

"If Jan ever gets tired of you, let me know. I'd grab you up in a second."

"Yeah, but only for a week."

Kay laughed until she cried. When she finally regained her composure she gasped, "Something tells me we'd last much longer than a week, Miss Evans. Much longer."

The next morning, Cole got up early and raced down the street for a newspaper. Shoving some change into the corner vending machine, she yanked the glass door open and grabbed a paper. She flipped to the front page of the local section and found the photograph, which occupied almost the entire top half of the page. She quickly glanced at the photo credit and smiled. In the lower left corner were the names "C.Evans/K.Stewart" in small bold print.

Cole was her own worst critic, but after scrutinizing the photograph from yesterday's fire even she conceded that it was good work. The entire burning building was visible. From the third-floor windows a funnel-like cloud of smoke billowed into the street. A firefighter was rescuing a man from the fourth floor, assisting him onto the extended fire ladder. Along the street, there were fire, police and rescue vehicles everywhere. People had gathered to watch the horrific scene from a distance, anxious for news of loved ones or simply magnetized by the destruction being wrought around them. It was Cole's best work — and she knew it.

Tucking the paper under her arm, Cole strolled back up the street to Tray's house. It was just after nine o'clock and Tray was awake and on the move. Uncharacteristically, she was already dressed and was bustling around the kitchen, making what looked to be breakfast.

"To what do I owe this honor?" Cole asked, sitting down at the kitchen table.

Tray smiled meekly. "I know, I know. Should make your breakfast every morning. You deserve it."

Cole waved her hand. "You never have to wait on me and you know it. Just wondered why you're on the go so early. Have an appointment or something?"

Tray cracked some eggs into a frying pan. "No, just a couple of surprises for you."

"Uh, surprises? Like what?"

Tray turned and smiled broadly. "Well, what do you think?"

Cole stared at her. Something was different, but she couldn't quite grasp what it was. "Think of what?"

"Cole, I can't believe you don't know. Look!" Tray pointed at her mouth.

Cole leaned forward. She couldn't believe her eyes. Magically, Tray had acquired a mouthful of teeth. "God, they look great. When did that happen?"

"I've had several appointments over the last two weeks. The molds had to be made. Picked 'em up yesterday. Like 'em, babe?" Tray stood in front of Cole and leaned over. "They're not the permanent ones, just a temporary bridge. See?" With a *click* and a *pop*, Tray had a handful of teeth.

"Amazing. But how?" Cole asked.

"With the money you lent me, babe. Only cost fifteen hundred bucks. Will tide me over 'til I get my case settled and can get new implants."

"You used the money I lent you to buy teeth?" Cole asked, in a slightly accusatory tone.

Tray frowned. Her words became defensive. "Yeah. Of course, babe. Can't exactly go on sales calls without any teeth. Could be what's been holdin' me back from gettin' these big accounts. You know how people can be."

Cole felt a severe pang of guilt. Tray's point connected immediately. Anyone in sales had to look and dress the part. Without teeth it must have taken Tray an enormous amount of guts to even walk into a prospective client's office. "I'm sorry. You did the right thing. Didn't mean to imply otherwise. A very smart move on your part."

"Thanks, babe. Knew you'd understand." Tray smiled again. "Have to think of it as an investment in my new business."

"That's a good way to look at it, yes. I think it's wonderful. You look fantastic."

Tray kissed her on the cheek. "How can I ever thank you? You've given me back my smile — the greatest gift anyone's ever given me." Tray threw her arms around Cole's neck. "I look in the mirror and guess what, Cole? I see me again. Have any idea what that means to me?"

Cole kissed Tray's neck. "You've got a beautiful smile, Tray. Keep flashing it and you'll have all the clients you can handle."

After breakfast Tray bounced up from her chair and said, "One more surprise, my love. Come with me. Out back in the alley."

Cole removed the napkin from her lap and placed it on her plate. She gazed toward the back door tentatively. "The alley?"

"Yes, the alley. Promise not to take unfair advantage of you."

Cole followed Tray through the kitchen's rear entrance. Walking through the small backyard, they quickly came to an unpaved alleyway. Just beyond the hedge that bordered the property was a narrow parking area. In it sat a beautiful black Firebird.

"Whose car is this?" Cole asked. "You should have it towed. It's on your property."

"Be kinda silly to tow my own car, wouldn't it?"

Cole was dumbfounded. "Your car?"

"Yeah, babe. New teeth, new car. Now I can get all over the city for my appointments. No more metro, no more worryin' about bein' late for an important meetin'. Now I can really impress my new clients. Take 'em to lunch even."

"You certainly have been busy," Cole said.

Patting the car lovingly Tray said, "Best thing is that I only put a few thousand bucks down on it. Still have plenty of money left to invest in the business and make the monthly payments. Once the money from the business starts rollin' in, maybe I can even take care of this broken down old house. Fix 'er up and make it into a real home for us."

"Seems like you're off and running, Tray. I'm very happy for you."

"None of it would've been possible without your help. I love you, Cole."

"Love you, too."

Tray opened the driver's side door. "Want to go for a spin?"

"Why not? Sounds like fun."

Closing the car door behind Cole, Tray rushed like a kid to the driver's side. A few minutes later, as they tore down the alleyway, barely missing the neighbor's trashcans, Cole closed her eyes and said a silent prayer. Cigarette dangling from her mouth, can of Mountain Dew between her legs and one hand on the steering wheel, Tray cruised the surrounding neighborhood in a speed-induced blur. Cole hung onto the dash as best she could without showing fear. As Tray veered from lane to lane and ran every yellow light at an unlawful speed, Cole couldn't help but think what she had set loose on the streets of Chicago. She also couldn't help but wonder what the weeks ahead would bring. Life with Tray had turned out to be eventful, to say the least. The nights and days were never boring. There were always more stories, surprises, new experiences and adventures. Cole thought back to her quiet life with Jan. As the next street passed in a blur, she wondered if her life would ever be quiet or settled again — and if that's the kind of life she really wanted.

Chapter Eight

A week and a half later, Tray was still racing around Chicago in her new Firebird with little success establishing any lucrative business prospects. Cole began to wonder what Tray really did all day. In the morning, Tray chain-smoked until about noon. For the rest of the day and into the evening, she was nowhere to be found. Tray claimed she was a night owl and did her best work in the afternoons and evenings. She called on potential business clients but never had any proposals, client information or tangible results to show for her efforts. She also exhibited an astounding lack of concern in light of these failures. For Cole, the weeks blurred together in a series of endless photo shoots and new worries. How was she going to pay her own bills — and Tray's mounting bills, too?

It was almost one in the morning. Cole had made her daily run to the newspaper, dropping off Friday's prints just before eleven o'clock. Instead of leaving right away, she'd hung out and worked with Marty, Donna and Barnes to test a new digital-processing system by developing some of her own photographs. All of them agreed that the results were excellent. The testing prompted Cole to rethink her hesitation to join the digital darkroom revolution.

While they were cleaning up the lab area where they had just worked, Sheila stopped in.

"Ah, I see you've all been trying out the new toys," she said cheerfully. "Good. The equipment's on loan until the end of next week and I'll expect a full report from all of you. Cost measured against results. Pros and cons of the process."

Marty wheezed and grunted. It was an affirmative reply.

"I think it's great you arranged for the trial period," Cole added.

Barnes laughed. "This coming from a staunch traditionalist. New surprises every day."

"Maybe old dogs can learn new tricks," Cole said, stooping down to store the chemicals underneath the sink bay.

"Well, we don't need to have a debate this minute," Sheila interrupted, leaning against the film cabinet. She was simply but attractively dressed in a coral blouse and white slacks. "Cole, can I have a word with you?"

Cole got up and untied her apron. "Uh, sure. What's up?"

Sheila led Cole into the hallway. "When are you going to come and work for us full-time? You promised me an answer and I still don't have one."

"I know. I'm sorry. I've been dealing with a lot of personal issues lately."

Sheila stared at her disapprovingly.

"Honest. Just give me a little more time. I've got some personal issues I really need to devote my full attention to right now."

"Is there anything I can help you with?"

"Just be patient for a little while longer."

Sheila sighed heavily and then forced an understanding smile. "Fortunately for you, Miss Evans, I am a patient person. I'll wait. But I want an answer by the end of next month. Fair enough?"

"Fair enough. Thanks."

Cole switched lanes and accelerated past a slow-moving Jeep. After a long day, she was tired — ready to soak in the tub and then hit the sack. Tray would probably still be awake, surfing the Internet. In addition to speeding around Chicago in her new Firebird looking for clients, Tray seemed to spend a lot of time on-line looking for the same with very few results. Cole couldn't quite figure it out. Tray's attempt to launch a business had run into roadblocks at every turn. She had shown Cole her business plan and it seemed sound. But each time Tray was about to land a big account, the opportunity vanished into thin air.

Just the other day, she and Tray had talked about the loss of another opportunity.

"These guys don't know what they're doin', babe. They pay three times as much a week for fresh-cut flowers and live plants in their lobbies, when they'd have a one-time cost for the silk arrangements and only have to replace 'em every few years," Tray complained, lighting another cigarette.

"The Holiday Inn?" Cole asked.

"No, the Ramada Inn."

Cole stopped listening. She stared at Tray, who seemed permanently glued to the same corner of the sofa. It was the exact spot Cole found her every morning. Each morning after she had showered and dressed for work, Cole would hustle down the steps to find Tray lounging on the sofa. Her legs were folded underneath her, cigarette in one hand, cup of coffee in the other, portable phone within reach. A nearby ashtray, heaped with cigarette stubs, was a permanent fixture. By eleven o'clock in the morning, Tray had accomplished nothing. She explained to Cole that she used the morning hours to make phone calls and plan her business objectives for later that day. Cole tuned Tray's voice back in, wondering if the woman would ever get a break.

"So, they finished lookin' at the price quotes and then I jumped in with another idea. For a few extra dollars a month, I offered to change out some of the flowers, dependin' on the season. You know, give the place a fresh look every couple a months."

"And . . ."

"Even made up a sample for them. Look." Tray removed the lid from a large, decorative box. From inside, she slid a beautiful silk floral arrangement resting in a large brass base. "The color scheme matches their lobby perfectly. Mauves and grays with white highlights here and here."

Cole blinked and stared, astounded by the talent Tray had exhibited in creating this striking accent piece. "Tray, it's gorgeous. Really. I'm very impressed. You have an incredible talent here."

"Thanks. Lotta good it's doin' me."

"Sounds and looks to me like they passed up a good deal."

"Just my luck," Tray said sarcastically. "But then we know my luck sucks."

Remembering this latest conversation, Cole shook her head. She had never met anyone like Tray — someone who was constantly dogged by crisis and personal turmoil. No matter what Tray said or did, it was preceded or followed by disappointment.

About a mile from her exit off Lake Shore Drive, Cole's beeper vibrated. She unclipped it from her belt. It was not a number she recognized. She quickly dialed the number from the car phone. A man's voice said, "Hello?"

"Hi, Cole Evans here. Did you beep me?"

"Cole, it's Hunt. Jackson's friend."

Cole was startled. Why would Hunt be calling her at one in the morning? "Uh, hello, Hunt. What's up?"

"Listen, I thought you'd want to know right away," he said, voice cracking. "There's been a fight. Jackson's badly hurt. He's at Bernard Mitchell now."

Panic tore through her. "Is he okay? What the hell happened?"

"He's in pretty bad shape. There was a fight

outside a gay club we went to tonight. David was involved, too. He's also at the hospital. I'll meet you there in a half-hour. Okay?"

"I'll be there." Cole disconnected the call and dialed Tray. The phone rang and rang. She was on the damned Internet. "Shit," she said out loud. At the next exit, she got off and then got back on heading north to 57th. As she executed the turnaround, she beeped Tray and waited for a callback.

After arriving at the hospital, Cole immediately found Hunt in the Emergency Center's waiting room. "Hunt! What's going on? You hear anything?"

Hunt was in his late twenties, Italian with dark hair and an olive complexion. Short in stature, he barely reached her shoulders, despite the leather dingo boots he wore with thick heels. He spoke excitedly, hands waving in the air, head jerking from side to side.

"Haven't heard nothing about Jackson, except that he's unconscious. They rushed him upstairs for testing." He pointed down the hall. "David's in one of the exam rooms being stitched up. He's got some ugly cuts on his face."

"What in the world happened?"

"They were attacked after they left JAM, a small gay bar south of here. That's all I know."

"Attacked by who?"

"Gang of teenagers. There were ten, maybe twelve of them. I blew outta the bar a little earlier than Jackson and David did. When I left, saw this group of kids hanging out across the street. Didn't like the looks of them — the way they glared at me, you know?

But my car was parked right out front. So I got in and drove away. David and Jackson left a few minutes later."

"Can we talk to David?"

"Yeah. Was just in with him. C'mon, I'll take you back." He took Cole by the arm and they half-ran down the hallway, dodging nurses, doctors, equipment and gurneys.

"Has someone called the police?" Cole asked.

"Uh-huh. David gave his statement. They're gonna come back and talk to Jackson later. Wanna ask him questions, too."

"I certainly hope so."

When they found David, he was sitting behind a curtained area on an examination table, head bowed, while a young intern stitched his scalp. The room smelled like a combination of rubbing alcohol and antiseptic spray. Cole put her hand on David's shoulder. "You okay?"

Without moving his head, he glanced sideways, his eyes glistening in the bright light. "Cole." He held her hand tightly. Multiple bruises had caused swelling along the right side of his face and his lip was split. There was dried blood on his chin and neck.

"He's okay," the intern said. "Another few stitches and we should be done. We'll give him some ice packs for the swelling and the bruises." The intern was standing to David's left, stitching the left side of his head. "There's not much we can do about that lip, I don't think. I might be able to put one or two stitches in it. Not sure yet."

"Thanks," Cole said, grabbing a stool and sitting in front of David. "What happened?"

"We got the shit beat out of us. That's what happened," he said angrily. His eyes were glassy, face contorted with pain. "Damn, it's all my fault. I wanted to take Jackson to meet a friend of mine who owns this small bar called JAM. Don't go there much anymore. Unfortunately, it's not in the greatest of neighborhoods."

"Doesn't matter where you went," Hunt interjected. "Shouldn't have happened anywhere. You know what I'm saying?"

"That doesn't change how I feel, Hunt. Ow!"

"Sorry about that," the intern said. "Small slip of the needle." He patted David on the shoulder. "We're done now anyway."

David waved him away. "It's okay. Thanks for your help."

"Let me take a look at that lip."

"No, it's okay. Really."

"It'll probably heal fine without stitches, so I'll stop torturing you for now." The intern slid the sterile worktable across the room. "I'll be back in a few minutes with some papers for you to sign."

"Okay, okay," David snapped. He turned to look at Cole. "What was I saying?"

"That it wasn't the greatest of neighborhoods," Cole answered.

"Oh, yeah. No, it's not. Don't know what I was thinking." David hopped down from the table and started to pace. "Jackson and I left the club just after Hunt. Maybe a few minutes. My car was parked about three blocks away. As we were walking to the car, I heard voices behind us. I felt this instant surge of adrenaline and swung around. There were about eight or so young kids walking behind us. This rush of panic came in a wave and I turned to Jackson and said, "I think we're in trouble. We have to decide now. Run or try to reason with them.' Jackson shot them a "don't mess with us' look and one yelled, 'Whaddaya lookin' at, faggot? C'mere, queer!' Jackson just looked at me and said, 'How fast can you run?' I didn't bother answering. We broke into a sprint and actually made it to the car. But they were too close behind. All of a sudden they were everywhere. Goddamn it!" David winced and put his hand to his head. "We tried to fight back, but we were obviously outnumbered. I concentrated on staying on my feet, afraid if I fell, they'd start kicking me. I was up against the car, and it was just one fist after another. Lots of yelling. 'Fag. Queer. Homo.' Someone must have heard the ruckus and called the cops. A cop car rounded the corner with lights flashing and all I could hear was footsteps running in every direction. Jackson was moaning. He was on the other side of the car on the ground. I stumbled over to him and he was covered in blood."

"Did the police catch any of them?" Cole asked hopefully.

"No. There were only two cops. They ran down the street with flashlights, but came back in about five minutes. They put out a call for an ambulance and that was it."

"Jesus," Cole mumbled. "You're both lucky to be alive."

"I asked the cops for a blanket to put over Jackson. It took them forever to find one. Then they just stood there and waited for the ambulance. They weren't particularly helpful. Or concerned, if you want to know the truth."

"Yeah, some hometown boys having a little fun on a Saturday night," Hunt said through his teeth. "Nothing to get excited about, you know? Whacking the shit out of a couple of queers ain't nothing."

"It's something," Cole said. "It damn well is something."

Cole and David waited anxiously in the hospital emergency room until just after six in the morning. During that time, Cole catnapped fitfully. She kept dreaming about Jackson when they were teenagers growing up in the same neighborhood. One night, when they were both fifteen, he had come over to her house well after midnight. It was the end of March. He positioned himself outside her second-story window, throwing pebbles at the glass. The tapping sound finally woke Cole up. When she peered outside, she saw the shadow of a person standing in the rain. She knew immediately who it was and unlatched the window.

"Jackson, what the hell are you doing?" she yelled, as the rain pelted her head and neck.

"Come down."

"It's after one in the morning. Are you crazy?"

"I need to talk to you."

Hearing the tremor in his voice, Cole threw on a

pair of jeans, sweatshirt and jacket and managed to sneak outside without waking anyone.

When she met him at the side of the house, his nose was bleeding and his lip swollen. Bleary-eyed, he stumbled into her arms. "Had a fight with my dad."

She hugged him tightly and kissed his stubbled cheek. "What happened?"

"Told him I was gay and he beat the crap out of me."

"C'mon, back to the garage," she said, starting in that direction. "It'll be warmer in there and we can talk."

Cole put her arm through Jackson's. He was limping along stiffly, as if in pain. In the garage, Cole dug out an army blanket from her father's old trunk. They sat on the metal trunk, huddled under the blanket. The musty fabric smelled like the garage — a mixture of oil and gasoline.

Cole pulled a rumpled tissue out of her jean pocket and wiped the blood away from Jackson's nose. "Are you okay?"

"He threw me out, Cole. Now what am I gonna do?"

Cole looked out the side window. In the glare of the backyard spotlight she could see that it was teeming rain. She could hear the drops pelting the garage roof and the rush of water pouring from the gutters just outside the door. "I think your mom will have something to say about that."

"She had her say. Stood there and let him do it."

"I can't believe that. She's crazy about you. You're all she ever talks about. Jackson this and Jackson that. She thinks you walk on water."

Jackson brushed the wet, matted hair away from his eyes. "Yeah, but she won't stand up to him."

"Probably not. Especially when he's in a mood like that. Maybe she thought it would make things worse for you if she said anything."

"Couldn't get much worse."

"How did it start?"

He shivered and his words came haltingly. "Was talkin' to a friend on the phone. All of a sudden my dad comes bustin' in my room, cussin' his head off. Says the coach of the football team, who's a drinkin' buddy of his, told him I was hangin' out with some of the 'fag' kids after school."

"Oh, brother," Cole said, rolling her eyes.

"Coach tells my dad I had my arm around one of 'em and that my dad better talk to me. That a lot of rumors were goin' around about me bein' queer." Jackson turned and looked at Cole. "Have you heard rumors about me?"

"No," she said, pulling the blanket up to her chin. "But no one in their right mind would say anything to me. Everyone knows we're best friends."

"Oh, yeah. Anyway, I got angry. I'm tired of hidin' how I feel. So I told him I was gay. I just blurted it out like a real dork." He dropped his head. "What was I thinkin'?"

"That he'd love and accept you anyway. That it wouldn't matter."

"So much for those stupid-ass ideas."

"My parents know about me. They're not thrilled, but they still love me. Still accept me and treat me halfway normal. Maybe you thought the same thing would happen."

"I can't go home, Cole. Do you think I could sleep here tonight?"

"In the garage?"

"Yeah, I'll be okay out here."

"No way. You come in the house. Sleep in the den. I'll leave a note for my parents so when they get up in the morning, they'll know you're in there and that everything's cool."

"Listen, I don't want to get you in trouble. I mean, my parents might call here or something. I can stay in the garage and leave before anyone gets up. No one will even know I was here."

"It'll be okay, Jackson. My parents are pretty hip about stuff like this. Besides, they really care about you."

"Well, if you're sure it's okay."

"It's okay. Honest." She grabbed his hand. "C'mon, I'm freezing to death out here."

A voice woke Cole from her dream. After a few seconds, her eyes began to focus. The voice turned out to be a doctor asking for Jackson's family.

"They live out of town, Doctor," Cole said groggily. She struggled to her feet. "I'm Jackson's friend, Cole Evans. This is another friend, David Tanner."

The doctor eyed them both. They must have looked like a sight. David's face was bandaged and bruised and he looked exhausted. Cole felt like a slug. Her clothes were wrinkled, her hair a mess, and she could barely focus her eyes. Cole forced a smile and, after a few moments, the doctor introduced herself.

"Dr. Anderson from neurology. Mr. Ward seems to be out of danger. Did a CAT scan and ruled out brain damage." The doctor tapped her pen on the metal

chart she was holding. "He did suffer a concussion —
a bruise of the brain, if that's more clear. We're
watching him very closely on that. Want to keep him
for observation for a few days. But I think the
prognosis, while somewhat guarded, is good. He's
resting comfortably now."

"When can we see him?" David asked anxiously.

The doctor checked her watch. "Visiting hours
start at nine o'clock. Mr. Ward has been moved to the
third floor. You can see him then."

Cole and David drank coffee, ate candy bars and
talked in the emergency waiting room until it was
time for visiting hours. They hopped on the elevator
to Jackson's floor and found his room a few minutes
later.

Despite the bandages around his head, oxygen tube
in his nose, bruises and swelling around his eyes, face
and neck, anyone would have thought that Jackson
was sleeping peacefully. His eyes were closed and his
hands were clasped, resting on his chest. The covers
were pulled up and folded neatly at his waist.

David stood on one side of the bed and Cole on
the other. Cole held Jackson's hand while David
stroked his forehead. She felt a lump forming in her
throat and fought back tears. He looked so goddamned
awful.

"You read about this shit every day," Cole finally
blurted. "But you never think it's going to happen to
someone you know."

David rubbed his eyes with his fists. "Why do we
think it's never going to happen to us?" He looked
over at Cole. "I should've known better. There's been
trouble at that club before. Trouble at other places in
the city just like this."

"Gay-bashing."

"Exactly. I guess beating the shit out of homosexuals is an amusing way to pass the night."

"Won't the police do anything? Patrol the neighborhoods?"

"Find a cop who cares and let me know," David said, clearly angry with himself. "It's my damned fault anyway. I'm the one who took him there."

Cole's beeper went off. She unclipped it from her belt and checked the number. It was Tray. "Be right back. Grab me in the hallway if he wakes up, okay?"

"Yes, of course," David mumbled, pulling a chair beside Jackson's bed.

As Cole headed toward the pay phone at the end of the hall, she felt her face flush with disappointment. She had tried to reach Tray hours ago and had never received a call back.

"Mornin', glory," the familiar voice drawled cheerfully. "Where you been? Workin' late?"

"No. I'm at the hospital. Didn't you get my page, Tray?"

"Yeah, just now. Worked real late and then fell asleep. Why? What's wrong? You okay?"

Cole sighed into the phone. A bomb could explode beneath Tray's bed and she would never wake up. One morning, while sitting in the kitchen eating breakfast, Cole had listened to Tray's alarm clock blare for more than thirty minutes. Finally, she couldn't stand it any longer and ran upstairs to shut it off. Several times, Tray had begged Cole to wake her up in time for an appointment. Cole would stand over her and call her name, rub her arm, jostle her. Nothing ever worked. She finally told Tray not to ask her to wake her anymore. It was too damned frustrating.

"I take it you didn't hear the beeper going off?" Cole asked, totally peeved.

"No, sorry. Why in the hell are you at the hospital? Talk to me!"

"I'm fine. It's Jackson. He got the crap beat out of him by a gang of teenagers outside a gay club."

"Is he okay?"

"He's still unconscious. But they've ruled out permanent brain damage, thank God."

"I'm glad to hear that."

Cole blinked back tears. "Wish you'd gotten the page. Really needed you."

"Sorry, babe. Besides, I don't know what help I could've been."

"You're a doctor, Tray! That would've helped. Plus, it's nice to have moral support when something like this happens. Kind of like the moral support I've been giving you."

Tray cleared her throat. "I'm sorry if I let you down, babe. Honestly. Listen, I'd drive there right now, but I've got some pretty important appointments today."

"On Saturday?"

"Businesses operate on Saturdays. I'll try to make it over there this afternoon."

"That's okay," Cole said coolly. "David's here. We're pretty much holding each other up. See you later. Bye." Cole hung up the phone before Tray could say anything else. She just wasn't in the mood to hear it.

Cole walked away from the pay phone and then

changed her mind. She swung around and dropped some more change into the phone. It rang about six times and then a breathless voice answered, "Hello?"

"Jan, it's Cole."

"Cole? Hi. Just came in from outside. Was at the store."

"Listen, I'm at the hospital. Thought you'd want to know that Jackson's been hurt. He's going to be okay, according to the doctors, but he's in pretty bad shape."

"Oh my God. What happened?"

"He was beaten by a gang." Cole finally lost it. She started to cry, but swallowed the tears. Her voice was shaky, but she managed to say, "He looks real bad, Jan."

"I'll be right down. Tell me the floor and the room."

Cole gave her the information. "Thanks, Jan. I appreciate it."

"Be there in twenty minutes."

Chapter Nine

Cole sat in the solarium just down the hall to give David some time to be alone with Jackson. The room was empty. She sat by the lone window, which had a beautiful view of that part of the city. She could see Washington Park just west of Cottage Grove Avenue. There was one big, looping pond that ran like a horseshoe around the park. It was a beautiful spring day and she imagined groups of kids roller-blading along the park's concrete walkways. She must have fallen asleep because the next thing she was aware of was a voice calling her name.

"Cole. Cole, wake up."

It was Tray, kneeling on the floor in front of her. "Sorry, I'm tired. Must have dozed off."

"You been up all night. No surprise you fell asleep. How's Jackson?"

"Okay." Cole sat up and stretched her cramped neck muscles. "Thought you had appointments. That you wouldn't be here until later."

"They can wait. Hell, they've waited this long."

"Thanks for coming. I appreciate it."

"No problem." Tray softly kissed Cole's hand. "Let's go see Jackson and I'll take a look at his chart, okay? Make sure they didn't miss anything."

"That would make me feel a lot better."

In the hallway, Tray stopped abruptly. "It feels kinda strange, if you want to know the truth. Bein' in a hospital again."

"Gosh, I was so worried about Jackson, I never considered how hard this might be for you. I'm sorry."

"It's okay. I'm fine. Had to happen sooner or later."

When they arrived at Jackson's room, he was still asleep. David had also fallen asleep, head resting on the bed's metal railing. He was jolted awake by the sound of their footsteps.

"David, Tray's here."

"Hi, Tray. Nice of you to come by," David said, rubbing his eyes.

"How you doin'?"

"I've been better. But okay."

Tray grabbed Jackson's chart from the end of the bed. She examined it for a couple of minutes, flipping through the three or four pages of notations. "His chart looks pretty good to me. They've got him sedated for pain. Probably why he's been sleepin' a lot. That and the head trauma. But no sign of serious brain injury. Just a mild concussion." Tray hung the chart back where she found it and then took Jackson's pulse. "Really, I think he's doin' fine. He needs rest. That's the best medicine right now."

"Thanks for checking. Makes both Cole and I feel better," David said politely.

"Glad to help out. They've got everything under control here. Besides, from everything I know, this is a damned good hospital."

"Hello, everyone." It was Jan, standing just outside the doorway. "May I come in?"

Tray's sudden appearance at the hospital had caused Cole to forget that Jan was on her way. "Jan, of course," Cole said sheepishly. "Uh, let me introduce you to everyone." Cole breathed deeply, trying to calm her nerves. She was glad Jackson was still asleep. The trauma of the present situation may have been more than he could stand. "This is Jackson's friend, David." Jan nodded in David's direction, then reached over and shook his hand. "And this is Tray Roberts."

Jan shot Cole a quick sideways glance. It was a disbelieving look. "Hi," Jan said coldly, glancing at Tray then back at Cole.

"Glad to meet ya," Tray said in her thick drawl. "Cole's told me a lot about you."

"I'll just bet she has," Jan said stiffly.

Tray approached Jan and put a hand on her shoulder. She smiled playfully. "Naw, really. I've heard all nice things."

"And I heard you're a doctor," Jan said, studying Tray with a good, long look. "How impressive. You must come in pretty handy for emergencies like this."

"I don't like meetin' people this way, but I try to be helpful when needed."

"Well, my real concern is for Jackson. Does someone mind telling me how he is?"

"I'll fill you in," Cole offered. "Let's get a soda or something, okay?" Cole motioned Jan toward the doorway. "Be right back," she said to the others.

Halfway down the hall, Jan practically spit the words into Cole's ear: "How could you?"

"I'm sorry. I didn't know you were both going to end up here at the same time. Tray wasn't supposed to get here until later this afternoon."

"Downright humiliating," Jan muttered. "I drop everything to come here and give you moral support. And what's my thanks for that? Meeting your new girlfriend!"

Cole stopped and grabbed Jan's arm. "Listen to me. Really, I'm sorry. I called because I knew you'd come and I needed you. I'm very grateful you're here."

"Was here. I've got to go."

"Please don't. At least stay long enough to have a soda with me in the cafeteria."

"I can't, Cole. I've got a million things to do."

"Okay. I understand."

"You'll keep me updated on Jackson?"

"Yes, of course."

"By the way, your new girlfriend doesn't look much like a doctor. Or act like one, for that matter."

"Why do you say that?"

"Listen, in my work as an interior designer you meet all kinds of people — develop an instinct about them." Jan looked down the hall toward Jackson's room. "And I developed one about her in approximately thirty seconds." Jan turned back to face Cole. "Watch yourself, Cole. Just some advice from an old friend."

Jan started to walk away, but Cole grabbed her arm. "Hey, hey. Wait a minute."

"Cole, I'm not in the mood for an argument, okay?"

"And you think I am? I've been here since one o'clock this morning scared out of my wits about Jackson. Now you're here telling me you've got this instinct thing happening with Tray."

"What do you care what I think?"

"I'd like you to explain yourself."

"Can't you see it?" Jan shook her head. "Maybe not. You're obviously too close to the situation."

"What are you talking about?"

"Take a good look at Tray, Cole. Listen to her. She's not educated. It's obvious. She talks like a hillbilly and looks like she just fell off a turnip truck, for God's sake."

"That's really a low blow. She's dressed casual because she rushed to get over here, just like you. And since when have you become such a snob? Just because Tray's got a Southern accent, doesn't mean she's not educated. People from the South do go to school."

"Fine, fine. Maybe it's me. I'm sorry. I have to get going."

Cole ended up in the cafeteria alone, sipping a Diet Pepsi. It was lunchtime and the room was bustling with activity. But the activity and the collective drone of conversation could not keep her from her own thoughts of Jan, her hurtful comments about Tray, and what had happened to their relationship.

Suddenly, she remembered the picnic. About a month after she and Jan had started seeing each another they planned a picnic together at Grant Park. It was the end of June, warm and sunny. A cool breeze drifted off the lake and tousled their blanket. Strategically, they weighted it down with the picnic basket and cooler. Sitting with a view of Buckingham Fountain, they watched the water shoot straight up and then spray outward from the force of the wind.

After a couple of months hanging out with the same crowd, Cole and Jan had decided to date "officially." For those two months, Cole could feel the attraction simmering between them. But so fearful of rejection, she waited for Jan to make the first move.

"Would you have ever asked me out?" Jan asked, biting into a strawberry.

Not really hungry yet, Cole ignored the food. She leaned back on her elbows, the sun warm on her face. "Uh, yeah. Sure. Just didn't know if you were interested."

"That's okay. I like the strong, silent type." Jan popped the rest of the strawberry into her mouth and stretched out next to Cole. The very short shorts she wore revealed already sun-bronzed thighs.

Cole hadn't dated in a little over a year. Her previous relationship had lasted six years and the hurt of the breakup still stung. Liz had left her suddenly, professing terrible unhappiness. In the months before meeting Jan, Cole had hung out with friends and was content just socializing and having fun without the worries of dating. Then she met Jan. Immediately, that spark of longing for the closeness of someone else was once again ignited. She had proceeded cautiously, however, loathe to screw it up.

"Uh, it's a beautiful day, isn't it?" Cole squinted into the sunlight. "There's nothing like summer in Chicago. Warm sun, cool breeze."

Jan threw her head back and laughed. "You're really nervous, aren't you?"

Cole laughed, too. "Slightly."

"I can tell. You're talking about the weather."

"Sorry. I think I've forgotten how to do this."

"Do what?"

"Date. Feel awkward."

"We've been seeing each other for a month, Cole. What's to be nervous about anymore?"

"I'm out of practice. Afraid to say or do the wrong things."

"You've done all the right things so far. Maybe this will help." Jan leaned forward and kissed Cole, the soft lips melting into her own. Cole could still taste the sweetness of strawberry as they wrapped their arms around each other and fell back onto the blanket. Cole's head touched the grass, the cool blades tickling the sides of her face. The kiss was long and sensuous, making her head spin. Running her hands down Jan's sides as they curved toward her hips, Cole languished in the touch of Jan's delicate skin. Suddenly, she didn't feel awkward anymore.

Jan ran her fingers through Cole's hair. "I think you're incredibly sexy."

"No, you're the one who's sexy."

"Is this going to be our first disagreement?"

"Uh-huh." Cole kissed Jan's cheek. "Not much of one, though, 'cause I know I'm right."

"How about a glass of champagne?"

Cole looked up into Jan's indigo eyes. Daylight made them sparkle, like two gems underneath glass. "Do we have any?"

"Not here. But I do back at my apartment." Jan smiled, tracing Cole's lips with her fingers. "We can have a picnic indoors. After all, it's a shame to waste a beautiful day like this."

"Trapped outside in this horrid park."

"Exactly."

The champagne hit Cole's empty stomach, giving her an immediate rush. She strolled around Jan's living room, amused, trying to take in all the fish. She and Jan had joked about it — a lesbian who loved fish. Seemed appropriate in a humorous sort of way. In the dining area was a 55-gallon tropical aquarium that gave the illusion of a small, peaceful underwater paradise. In the living room a large, metal sculpture of angelfish dominated the wall. There were other fish sculptures and wall hangings and seashells in glass jars. Cole chuckled and sipped her champagne.

The soft fingers and long nails brushing against the nape of her neck almost made her drop the glass. Cole turned to find Jan dressed only in a camisole and panties.

Jan took the glass from Cole's hand and drank some champagne. "Mmmm. Good." She pressed up against Cole, her skin hot, her kisses soft against Cole's neck. "I can't wait for you to fuck me. I'm wet and ready for you," she whispered into Cole's ear.

Cole tried to swallow the lump in her throat. She

opened her mouth to say something. Exactly what, she didn't know. But before any words could be uttered, Jan slipped her tongue inside Cole's mouth.

Cole lifted Jan into her arms and set her down on the waist-high counter that divided the kitchen from the living room. Caressing Jan's hips, she rolled her panties away and kissed the soft skin of her stomach. She could feel Jan's fingers in her hair, the long nails gently scraping along her scalp, down her shoulders and over her back. Cole buried her face between Jan's thighs and lovingly stroked her until she heard her sighing deeply. Jan's legs opened wider for Cole, her nails digging into Cole's back.

"So sweet," she whispered in a short, quick gasp. Then Jan's body stiffened and she cried out, her hips quivering beneath Cole. "Darling," she whispered. "I love you."

Cole wrapped her arms around Jan's waist. "I love you, too."

Jan sat up, wrapped her legs around Cole's waist and let Cole lift her to the floor. Rolling on top of Cole, Jan straddled her, pulling Cole's fingers inside. As Jan thrust herself downward against her hand, Cole caressed Jan's breasts. She covered them with soft kisses, ran her tongue across hard nipples, took in the scent of Jan's sweet, flowery perfume. And when she felt Jan come again in her arms, she gave her heart and lost herself in the lingering moments that followed.

The clatter of dishes and mingled conversation pulled Cole back to the present. Suddenly, she was once again aware of the hospital, Jackson's beating, Jan meeting Tray, the ugly words exchanged with Jan. She dropped her head onto the cafeteria table, the cold laminated surface pressing into her forehead. She sobbed. She didn't care who heard her.

Chapter Ten

The following weekend, the children in the dialysis center squealed with delight when the Saturday show ended. They clapped and gathered around Cole, wanting to see the *Sesame Street* puppets and her magic hat. Although Cole felt like she had spent an eternity in the hospital since Jackson's beating, she patiently talked with the children while Jan packed up most of the equipment.

On the way out of the center, Jan paused along the sidewalk in front of the building and faced Cole.

From the time Cole had picked her up that morning until now, Jan had barely uttered a word.

"Cole, I want to talk to you about something."

Cole squinted into the sunlight. "What?"

Jan folded her arms across the hunter green sweater vest she was wearing over a yellow oxford cloth shirt. "First of all, I want to apologize for what I said the other day about Tray. That was really unfair. I'm not proud of it, but I guess I was trying to hurt you."

"Forget about it."

"Thanks. Second, your bank called and left a message about the loan you recently applied for. You're supposed to call them back as soon as possible. I have the name and number of the person you're to call." Jan held out a piece of paper. It flapped in the breeze.

"Uh, okay," Cole said, reaching for the slip of paper.

"Why did you need a loan? Are you and Tray buying a house together?" Jan's lips were trembling. Her voice was shaky. "Are you gone out of my life for good?"

Cole felt an immediate need to reassure Jan. She put her hands on Jan's shoulders. "No, no. That's not it at all. I'm not buying a house."

Jan looked away. "Then why did you need a loan? I don't understand."

"Uh, it wasn't a loan for me."

"What do you mean, not a loan for you?" Jan asked, looking back, eyes boring into her.

"I borrowed the money to lend to someone else."

"Who?"

"Uh, Tray."

"Why did you loan money to Tray?"

Cole moved to the edge of the sidewalk to let an older woman and a dog pass. "She needed it to start a business."

"I thought you said she was a doctor, for God's sake."

"Used to be a doctor," Cole explained. "She was disabled in a bad accident some months ago. She can't practice medicine anymore."

"She looked fine to me."

"Listen, she needed the money, okay?"

"How much did you lend her?"

"She's going to pay me back. It's no big deal."

"How much, Cole?"

Cole hesitated and then said, "Fifteen thousand dollars."

"Fifteen . . ." Jan stopped abruptly and stared at Cole in disbelief. "Fifteen thousand? Cole, what were you thinking? What could you possibly have been thinking?"

"That I wanted to help someone I care about."

Jan's black loafer began tapping against the cement sidewalk. "Well, I hope you had enough sense to get her to sign some legal papers or something."

Cole sighed. "Tray's having the papers drawn up now. She insisted on it, as a matter of fact."

"You already gave her the money without having her sign a loan agreement? Are you crazy?"

"No, I trust her."

Jan's voice cracked with anger. "Well, I don't. In fact, I withdraw my earlier apology. I don't trust that woman one bit. There's something really shady about her. I think she's using you, Cole, if you really want to know the truth."

"Listen, you don't have to trust her. She's not

using me and there's nothing strange about her other than she's had some difficult times lately. I think you're jealous. That's what's really at the root of this."

"Jealous?" Jan raised her eyebrows. "Well, you may be right about that. But that doesn't mean I don't have justifiable concerns for you. You've known this woman all of four months and you go and hand her fifteen thousand dollars for some business she's trying to start?" Jan shifted her weight from one foot to the other. "Excuse me if I'm a bit jaded in concluding that you may not have given enough thought to this. That you may have acted emotionally rather than, shall we say, rationally?"

"Doesn't matter why I did what I did," Cole mumbled. "It was my decision, not yours."

"You're right. It's not for me to say what you should do with your money. I just hate to see you get hurt."

"That's an interesting remark, coming from you."

"Have I hurt you that much?"

"Yes."

"I'm sorry. That was never my intention. I thought if I concentrated on myself for a while that it would help our relationship by making it stronger." Jan rubbed her forehead with her hand, staring at the pavement. "Instead, all I succeeded in doing was hurting us both. What a terrible mistake I've made. I never wanted to lose you, Cole. But now I have, haven't I?" Jan turned and started to walk away. "You don't have to drive me back. I'll catch the subway," she yelled over the street traffic.

Jan's short, quick steps pounded against the pavement and eventually faded at the end of the block until she was no longer in sight. Walking in the opposite direction, Cole shoved her hands into the pockets of her jacket. It seemed that they were always moving in opposite directions now, miles and miles apart from each another.

Later that afternoon, Cole stopped by Jackson's apartment to check on him. He had been released from the hospital, but had not yet been cleared to return to work.

With the extra key Jackson had given her, Cole let herself into the apartment.

"Jackson? Hey, where are you?"

"Upstairs," came the faint reply.

He was still in bed. He was sitting up, trying to eat a bowl of Jell-O. "Damned," he said, dropping the Jell-O down the front of his T-shirt. "Did they have to stomp on my hands? They're still so fuckin' sore, I can barely use them." He threw the spoon down. It landed on the tray-table and bounced onto the floor.

"Here, let me help you," Cole said. She picked up the spoon and cleaned it off. Scooping up some Jell-O, she offered it to him.

He flashed a look of disgust, then begrudgingly accepted. "If I weren't starving to death, I'd send you home."

"Is that any way to talk to your best friend?"

"Sorry. I'm in an ill mood today."

"I don't blame you."

"Everything's sore — and I do mean everything. If I had an Uzi, I'd mow all those bastards down. Never give it a second thought."

"Eat some more Jell-O."

Jackson swallowed with some difficulty. "Cole, you remember when we were kids? Junior high school?"

"Sure I remember."

"Remember that real feminine guy?" Jackson closed his eyes. "Can't think of his name right now."

"Scott something."

"Yeah, Scott. How all the kids used to mock him, call him 'faggot' and 'fairy' and all that. They tormented the hell out of that kid and I remember thinking, because even then I sort of knew about myself, that if I had to go through that shit, I'd kill myself and get it over with."

"Terrible what some of these kids go through. And a lot of them are suicidal."

"I thanked God every day that I was masculine-looking and good at sports. That's why I went out for every sports team there was, you know."

"I know."

"I thought if I was Mr. Jock, no one would ever question me. And it worked. At least for a while. Who'd have thought that as an adult, a grown man, I'd have to go through this kind of crap and humiliation?"

"I think it happens a lot. More than we know. Look what happened to that poor guy in Wyoming. Beaten and left to die like that. Makes me sick."

Jackson hung his head. "I know. What the hell am I complaining about? Should consider myself lucky, I guess."

"I think you and David were 'lucky' in that you weren't both killed. But you certainly have a right to complain. No one deserves to be beaten within an inch of their life."

"No one cares. That's the bottom line. If I were dead, maybe they'd be looking a little harder for these guys." Jackson caressed Cole's cheek. "I'm sorry this has upset you so much."

"Of course it has. I love you."

"I know. And I thank God for that." Jackson smiled and winced at the same time. He put his hand to his head and massaged his temples. "I've been worried about you."

"You can stop worrying, Jackson. I'm fine."

"Really?"

"Yes, really. Speaking of being fine, I'd be a hell of a lot more fine if you'd get your ass out of this bed and get back to your life outside this apartment. I miss trouncing your butt at darts."

"Trouncing my butt? Oh, brother, listen to you. Well, then you'll have to feed me some more Jell-O. Got to get my strength back."

Cole leaned over and kissed Jackson on the forehead. "Tried to find a spot that didn't look sore."

"You have a spot. Right here." Jackson pointed to his heart. "That's where you'll always be."

Monday evening, Cole relaxed after dinner. Still sitting at the kitchen table, she read *Curve* magazine while Tray made some fresh coffee.

"Did you enjoy dinner?" Tray asked, reaching for the creamer.

"Sure did. The steaks were great."

"You bought 'em. The least I could do was cook 'em."

"Thanks. Appreciate it. I enjoy having dinner

together when my schedule with the paper isn't so crazy."

"Like havin' you around, babe."

"I sure hope so."

Tray poured herself some coffee and pointed to the mug. "Want some?"

"No, thanks. I'll be up all night."

"How 'bout some hot chocolate?"

"Now you're talking."

A few minutes later, they were both sipping their drinks.

"Tray, did you ever get those loan papers from your lawyers? We should get them signed, you know."

Tray hit her forehead with the palm of her hand. "I know, babe. I know. Meant to say something earlier. Just called their office today and couldn't get through. They've got some big case that just went to trial. Sorry."

"That's okay," Cole said uneasily. Recently, she had started doubting Tray's promise to have loan papers prepared by her aunt's estate lawyers. Weeks had passed and there were still no papers. But lawyers were known for taking their own sweet time.

"Honest, babe. I plan to hound the hell out of 'em all week. Damn, I'm sorry."

"No problem. Just so we get it resolved soon."

"You have my personal promise on that."

"It's not that I don't trust you, Tray. The legal documents are just for my protection. Suppose, God forbid, something happened to you? How would I be reimbursed?"

"No, no. You're absolutely right. This needs to be done pronto." Tray smiled and lit a cigarette.

"Wouldn't want anyone to think I was tryin' to take unfair advantage of you."

"I don't care what other people think. And I don't think that."

"That's all that matters to me." The end of the cigarette flashed red and smoke swirled into the air, mixing with the cooking smells. Tray glanced at the cover of *Curve*, then said, "Hey, I almost forgot. Have a present for you." She pulled a piece of paper out of her front shirt pocket and slid it across the table.

Cole picked it up and recognized it as the business card she had seen in its preliminary design stages. Looking newly printed it read: Tray Roberts, Design Consultant and Owner, Dream Decor Unlimited.

"Well, whaddya think?" Tray asked, dumping another spoonful of sugar into her coffee. "They're hot off the presses."

"This turned out really nice. Can I keep it?"

"Sure, babe. Saved the very first one for you."

"Thanks." Cole tucked the card into her wallet.

"You might want one of these, too."

Cole eyed the glossy paper as it slid across the table. "Your brochure! Hey, this looks great. Very professional."

"My friend, the one I told you about at dinner that night. With David and Jackson?"

"Yes, I remember."

"She did such a super job. Got me a great deal on the printing, too."

"Well, you're certainly in business now. Say, how's the Internet research coming along?"

"Not bad. Tryin' to negotiate some decent prices with silk floral suppliers. Buyin' in bulk gives me an edge over the long haul. Just haven't cut the right deal yet."

"What about a Web site?"

"Now that's an entirely different story. I've been lookin' into it, but it's a little more complicated than I thought. Been playin' around with some very early designs and ideas, but I might need some help from someone who knows what they're doin'."

"Maybe your friend can help. The same one who did the brochure."

"Yeah, she's a real computer whiz, too. Said she'd help me out, no charge. I'm gonna hand her cards out when I call on clients."

"Seems like a fair exchange."

"Yeah, we think so. But for now, I think the bulk of my money's gonna be made from poundin' the streets and hopefully landin' some big commercial accounts. The Web site design might take a little longer."

"Once you get the accounts, where are you going to fill the orders?"

"Hey, that's the beautiful part of this thing, babe," Tray said, putting down her coffee cup. "So little overhead. My flower factory ain't gonna cost me nothin'. Gonna use the basement. It's got plenty of good light and all the space I need. The only thing I've gotta do is install some shelvin' and a large worktable. That way, I can put the majority of my capital into materials and shippin'."

"Right now, the basement's pretty much a mess."

"No shit. I'm havin' a yard sale this weekend. Gonna sell all that old stuff. Clear out the basement so next week I can set up shop. Gotta be ready to start fillin' orders. I just know I'm gonna break in some business real soon."

"Well, I'd be more than happy to help."

"Thanks. I feel like I've got a million things on my mind. It's all happenin' too slowly for me."

"These things take time. Starting a new business is no small task."

Tray gulped some coffee. "Tell me about it." Tray got up and refilled her mug. "Listen, I gotta go do some work on-line. Have a couple of suppliers I need to contact."

"Okay. I'll clean up the dishes."

Tray kissed Cole on the forehead. "I'll be workin' late, but if you can manage to wait up for me, it would be a great way to end the day."

"I've got the night off and a good book to read. I'll wait."

"Love you."

"Love you, too."

Cole cleared the dishes and put them in the dishwasher. She also sorted through the mess on the kitchen counter. Unopened mail was stacked in every corner. Mail that had been opened was in its own disorganized heap. Post-it Notes and scraps of paper with hurried scribbles were stuck or taped to the cutaway above the counter. Cole thumbed through the bills and separated them from the countless letters from Tray's attorneys. Then she bound the unopened mail together with a large rubber band, piling it neatly by the phone. She grabbed the stack of opened mail, and a letter on top suddenly caught her attention. It was from the Department of Health and Human Resources, Social Security Administration. It read:

Dear Ms. Roberts,
Please have your physician fill out the attached
health report in order that your disability claim
may be renewed for an additional year with the
Department of Health and Human Resources. A
brief summary of your claim history is detailed
below:

Date first applied for disability status:
November 15, 1996.
Reasons: Epilepsy.
Statement by claimant: Loss of memory, cannot
drive, bumps into things, gets lost on public
transportation, hard of hearing, right side
numb, has trouble writing, cannot under- stand
simple instructions, gets confused easily.
Medication: Dilantin.
Other conditions: Loss of teeth because cannot
afford dental work.

Cole stopped reading. There had to be some
mistake. According to Tray, she had only been disabled
about nine months. Cole read the date again:
November 15, 1996. If this letter was accurate, Tray
had been disabled and on government assistance for
years.

Cole put the letter and attachment back on top of
the pile where she found them. Had Tray lied about
her work and disability history — as well as her
assertion that she'd been a doctor? According to Tray,
she had worked at Grady Hospital in Atlanta for two
years up until the car accident nine months earlier.
On an impulse, Cole grabbed the letter and headed

upstairs to confront Tray. She felt an instant need for clarification.

At the doorway to the den, Cole hesitated. Tray was typing with two fingers, a lit cigarette dangling from her mouth. The ashtray on the desk was already half full and the small room was clouded in smoke. Cole noticed that Tray was communicating with someone via instant message.

"Who are you talking to?" Cole asked.

Clearly startled by the intrusion, Tray swiveled the chair around and took the cigarette out of her mouth. "Hey, babe. You shouldn't sneak up on someone like that."

"Who are you talking to?" Cole persisted.

"A supplier," Tray answered harshly. "He's been quotin' me some pretty good prices."

"Tell him to hang on. I need to ask you a question."

Tray glanced at the papers Cole held. She typed a few words into the instant message box on the screen and then said, "Okay. What's so important that you'd interrupt a potential business deal?"

Tray's attitude conveyed an air of superiority which more than irked Cole. "I was cleaning up the kitchen and found this letter from the Social Security Administration. Says you've been disabled since nineteen-ninety-six."

Tray started to laugh. Blowing a cloud of smoke into the bigger cloud hanging over her head, she laughed some more.

"What's so funny?"

Tray leaned back in her chair and crossed her legs. She had a smug look on her face. "Babe, have you ever had any dealings with the Federal government?"

"Just to pay my income taxes," Cole said in an annoyed tone.

"Well," Tray said, throwing her hair over her shoulder, "I hope you never have to go through the red tape and aggravation I've been through." Tray pulled her wallet from her jeans pocket. "See the social security number on the top of that sheet you're holding?"

Cole glanced down at the paper. "Yes. What about it?"

"Take a good look at it, then take a look at this."

Tray handed Cole a card. It was her social security card. The number on her card and the number on the letter were completely different. Cole was utterly confused. "What's the deal here?"

"They've got my ass mixed up with someone else's, Cole. Know how many Tracy Robertses are out there? Since my brief history of dealin' with the government personally, I've found out there are quite a few Tracy Robertses scattered across the country."

Cole felt an instant surge of remorse for her suspicions. "I'm sorry. Got confused when I read the letter. Couldn't understand how this could possibly be you."

"That's because it ain't me." She grabbed the papers from Cole and quickly scanned them. "First of all, I don't have epilepsy. Second, I don't get lost on public transportation. Good thing, too — especially when you live in Chicago." Tray chuckled again and shoved the papers back into Cole's hands. "The only thing this person and I've got in common is bad teeth. Unfortunately, mine got knocked out in an auto accident."

"Well, you're right. You certainly aren't in the

condition described here." Cole pointed to the document. "This person sounds like she's practically an invalid. Like I said, I couldn't imagine that this was you."

Tray nodded and smiled. "Glad you gave me the benefit of the doubt."

Cole shrugged and backed out of the doorway. "Sorry to have bothered you. I'll let you get back to your work. Good luck with your supplier."

"If I still have one."

Cole lay awake for a long time, waiting for Tray. But Tray never came to bed. After what had happened, Cole really couldn't blame her. She had questioned Tray's integrity and honesty. After everything Tray had been through in the past months, Cole could understand why Tray was upset with her. Cole tossed and turned until, completely exhausted, she fell into a restless sleep.

Late the next morning, Cole was surveying another murder scene. According to the cops, who seemed more than willing to give Cole the inside scoop, the murder was drug-related and had happened about half an hour earlier. In broad daylight, two young men were gunned down in a drive-by shooting. Police were still interviewing eyewitnesses, neighbors and those unlucky enough to have been in the vicinity when it happened.

Cole worked the perimeter of the area, clicking off photos from every conceivable angle. It was a bloody, violent scene that left her sickened. After all the violence she had witnessed in her work as a photographer, there were still incidents that had the power to shock and sadden her.

"What a mess. Not a good way to start the day."

Cole turned to find Kay Stewart standing behind her. "Kay! Yes, it's a mess. Amazing only two people were killed the way this area was sprayed with bullets."

Kay pointed to the house in front of them. "Look, they even shot out the first-floor windows, those bastards. They had to rush that entire family to the hospital. They're all in shock, including two little ones."

Cole shook her head in disbelief. "Well, I'm done here. What about you?"

"More than done. Want to grab a cup of coffee?"

"Yes, that would be great. I missed my morning cup when I got beeped here."

"C'mon, then. We'll take my car."

A few blocks away, Kay parked near a small breakfast and lunch café. Inside, it was airy and cool with the aroma of coffee and pastries and the sound of small talk from patrons. They sat at a round table near the front window. It had a view of the bustling, inner-city neighborhood.

Kay bought them each a cup of coffee and a Danish. "My treat. We don't get to do this too often."

"Thanks, Kay. No, we don't — as much as we sometimes run into each other." Cole unwrapped her Danish and cut it in half, happy to be in the reassuring company of her friend.

Kay sipped her coffee, staring over the rim of the cup at Cole. Her wide shoulders and large frame were leaning forward, elbows resting on the table. "What you been up to, Cole? How's Jan? Never see her anymore."

Inwardly, Cole shuddered. She hated having to answer that inevitable question. But it was time to come clean with Kay. She felt guilty for not having told her sooner. "Uh, well, I guess in the excitement of our last meeting it slipped my mind to tell you. Jan and I aren't a couple anymore."

Kay's deep green eyes were full of questions. "Slipped your mind to tell me? What the hell happened?"

"Lots of stuff. No one's fault, really."

"Gosh, that surprises me, girl. Thought you made such a fabulous couple."

"I thought so, too."

"I take it the demise of your relationship wasn't mutual."

"No. I loved Jan. Still do."

"I'm sorry." Kay squeezed Cole's arm. "Listen, I know I tease about how attracted I am to you, but I really am sorry, Cole."

"Thanks." Cole took a bite of her Danish. A blob of raspberry filling plopped onto the table. Wiping it up, she glanced out the window. The skies were clearing and the sun was breaking through. "I'm seeing someone new," Cole blurted. She hadn't been sure whether to share the information or not.

"Well, good for you," Kay said enthusiastically. "Hate sad stories. But now the story's taken a turn for the better. Anyone I know?"

"Don't think so. Her name's Tray Roberts."

"Tray Roberts? Hmmm, why does that name sound strangely familiar?"

"Don't know. She hasn't lived here that long. Nine months or so."

"Oh, then I guess it's not the same person. Thought I'd met someone by that name — but it's been quite a while. Seems to me the woman I'm trying to remember wasn't held in very high regard. Had a bad reputation as a use-'em-and-lose-'em type." Kay cut into her pastry with a plastic fork. "I've got a good memory for a face, but names are a weakness."

"Well, Tray's a great person. She's had some hard times lately, but I think her luck's about to change. At least I hope so."

Kay studied her for a few moments. "Everything okay?"

"I don't know. Tray and I have been seeing each other since February. She's really been through a lot and I've been trying to help her get back on her feet."

"That's you, Cole. I can't imagine you doing anything less."

"Trouble is, I've been feeling so guilty lately."

"Why?"

"I've started to have these nagging doubts. About who Tray really is and what her true motives are. Then I chastise myself for being suspicious. I start feeling like a creep."

"What do you mean you question her motives?"

"Never mind. Long story."

"Listen, if you want to talk, Cole, you've got my home and work phone numbers. You call me if you need me."

"Thanks. Enough about me. What's happening in your life?"

Kay put her muscled arms behind her head and stretched. "Oh, not much. I go out with friends, do a little socializing. Occasionally, I date someone. But as you know, I keep pretty much to myself. Try to avoid complications."

"Uh, yes. There's something to be said for that. I haven't always agreed with your philosophy of isolationism, so to speak. But I may be changing my tune in my old age."

"Naw. You only feel that way now because of what's happened with Jan. You'll be fine. Just give it some time."

"Maybe." Cole added some more cream to her coffee. It was strong. "But don't you ever get lonely? I do wonder about that."

"Not really. I've got some great friends. They'd never let me be lonely. Would pound on my door and ring the phone off the hook before that ever happened."

"Then you're lucky. You've got some very good friends who obviously care about you."

"Hey, I'm their main form of entertainment. The life of every party."

Cole laughed. "I can see that."

"Listen, we've got to stop meeting like this. It'd be great if you and Tray could join me and my illustrious group of friends one evening for dinner and some dancing."

"I'd like that. Would love to meet some of your friends. And, we haven't danced together lately," Cole said with a coy smile.

"No, we haven't. Besides, then I can check out Tray and see what kind of vibes I get." Kay finished her coffee and threw her crumpled napkin inside the paper cup. "Too bad I didn't know you were available, Miss Evans. Might've snapped you up myself," Kay said, with a mischievous grin. "But only for a week, of course."

Cole laughed from deep within. She felt embarrassed, but tried to accept the compliment graciously. "That was a nice thing to say. At least I think so."

"It was meant in the kindest possible way. Ready to face the world again?" Kay asked, pushing her chair away from the table. "Gotta get back to the office. Lots of lab work to do."

"Yes, I'm ready. Hey, thanks for treating me to brunch."

"Anytime. And I'll call you next week about getting together, okay?" Kay put her arms around Cole's shoulders and gave her a warm hug. She kissed Cole's cheek softly and moved away. "Remember, if you need to call and talk, please feel free."

Chapter Eleven

The view from Navy Pier was like the picture postcards Cole had seen at every tourist stop in Chicago. It was a beautiful June day and Tray and Cole had decided to spend Saturday down at the pier. It was crowded with natives and tourists trying to enjoy the seventy-degree weather.

Navy Pier was Chicago's number one tourist attraction — and for good reason. It had been constructed in the early 1900s as an entertainment area, especially in the summer when festivals drew hundreds of thousands of people.

Cole and Tray sat in the outside section of Charlie's Ale House, sipping one of the pub's seventy different beers before their sandwiches arrived. From the alehouse they had a great view of the shoreline and the various water taxis that ferried tourists out onto Lake Michigan.

"Great idea to come out here, babe. Beautiful day," Tray said, adjusting her sunglasses.

"Yes, it is." Cole stared at the sunglasses and inwardly seethed. They were another new purchase by Tray, who had yet to realize one dime of income from her new business. Another entire month had passed and Tray's venture seemed no closer to the launching stage. The basement hadn't been cleaned out — and not a single floral arrangement had been made. Ill with a sinus infection and cold for the past two weeks, Tray had lounged well into the afternoon hours each day, accomplishing nothing. She had managed, however, to drag herself out dancing until the early-morning hours at least three or four times during this bout of illness. Tray claimed that, due to her aunt's murder and all the legal red tape, she had lost touch with friends and needed to reestablish some personal contacts. During the daylight hours, Tray said she spent the past two weeks getting her strength back and rearranging appointments with potential clients. They were insincere excuses that didn't ring true.

Cole had been supplementing Tray's finances for months. It was beginning to take both an emotional and a financial toll. She had been paying all the utility bills to keep Tray's aunt's house afloat, plus a number of other debts that had resulted in calls from creditors three or four times a day. Tray refused to talk to the creditors and Cole was sick of listening to the messages left on the answering machine. She had finally begun to lose her patience.

"Tray, I'm tired of waiting for your lawyers to draw up those loan papers." Cole waited for a reaction to this announcement and got none. Tray's mirrored sunglasses reflected only the water, hiding those expressive eyes. "So I had my own lawyer draw up a loan agreement. It's back at the house and I'd like you to review it by the end of the week. Then we'll stop by a notary and sign it. Okay?"

Tray bit into her roast beef sandwich. She stared at Cole, then wiped a drop of mayonnaise from her chin. "Sorry about the loan papers. My lawyers are finally settling my aunt's estate. They've been a bit tied up."

"The estate's being settled?"

"Yeah. The murder's still unsolved. Probably always will be. Unfortunately, my aunt will be nothing more than an empty statistic. Kinda disturbing."

"She'll always be much more than that to you."

"I think so. Someone who helped me when I needed it most. Like you."

"I've tried."

"You've done much more than that. We can sign your lawyer's papers, no problem. I'm sure I can get to them by the end of the week. Now that I'm feelin' better, I've been busy settin' up client appointments and finally gettin' ready for the yard sale. Need to clear out the basement pronto."

"I understand, Tray. I'd just like to get the documents back to my lawyer as soon as possible."

"And you will." Tray cupped her hands, struck a match and lit a cigarette. Cole watched as the smoke trailed into the breeze, thinking that it was an expensive habit Tray could ill afford. "Babe, how many times have I told you that everythin' I have right now I owe to you? Payin' you back is a responsibility I take very seriously." Resting her cigarette in an ashtray, Tray took another bite of her sandwich. "You're first on the list to be paid back," she said through a mouthful of food. "Don't you worry, babe. Not payin' you back ain't an option. Love you, respect you and am too grateful to ever let that happen."

Cole's gaze wandered toward the water. Tray always had a knack for making her feel guilty and somehow responsible for things she had little control over. But that tactic was finally wearing thin, too. "I appreciate that, Tray. I've told you before, you can pay me back over time or you can assume the loan payments. Whatever's easiest for you."

"Not a problem," Tray said, shaking her head. "You'll be written one check with interest that'll take care of everything."

Cole brushed some wind-blown hair from her eyes. "Whatever you say."

Reaching across the table, Tray grabbed her arm. "Listen to me, Cole. I'm serious as a heart attack here. What I want's for you to understand how much you mean to me. How grateful I am for everything you've done. Maybe I don't tell you enough. But I do love you and I know I'm lucky to have you in my life." Tray dropped the napkin onto her plate and pushed it away. "I've been so messed up lately. Hard to get a grip on all the shit that's happened to me in the past ten months." The volume of Tray's voice dropped until Cole could barely hear her. "When everything comes together — the business, the financial stuff, all the lawyers outta my hair — I want to concentrate on us, Cole. That's what's most important anyway. The rest of this stuff ain't nothin' to me. But you, you're everything."

Cole squinted into the sun, smiled and tried very hard to believe. "Uh, glad to hear you say that, Tray. No matter what the future brings — even if we end up just being friends — I want you to be happy. I'd like to think that this new start you're making with your life will lead to only good things for you."

"Thanks to you, I know it will." Tray squeezed Cole's hand. "Guess what I'm doin' Monday, babe?"

"What?"

"Pickin' up all my silk-flower supplies. Finally, after all these weeks of hasslin' with wholesalers, I found one that met the price I wanted. Now I can finally start fillin' orders."

"What orders?"

"My friend who know computers? She's helpin' me to design a Web site, Cole. Plus, I'm closin' in on some big accounts. In fact, I'm drawin' up a contract for the Holiday Inn tonight. They called me yesterday and want me to do some preliminary work for them. That means cash flow, Cole. Can you believe it?"

Cole felt a surge of relief. She had begun to think it would never happen. "Best news I've heard in weeks. Congratulations."

"C'mon, let's take a walk."

Tray held Cole's hand as they walked the full length of the pier until it ended with a panoramic view of Lake Michigan. Cole had been told that on a clear day, from the top floor of the Hancock Building behind them, the shores of Wisconsin could be seen across this vast, blue space. From this vantage point, the lake seemed endless. The water appeared to blend with the sky, giving the illusion of even greater expanse, which wasn't really an illusion at all.

"Well, Kentucky ain't got nothin' to match this, I'm afraid," Tray said with a chuckle. "Kinda humblin', ain't it?"

"It really is."

"I felt that way about medicine, too. The science of it, the miracle of healin'. It could humble the hell outta you."

"Humility isn't a bad thing. Keeps you honest."

"So does love. It humbles you, too. In a nice way. And I do love you, Cole."

"I love you, too."

Cole slid the print into the fixer. She agitated the tray and studied the image. It was a picture she had taken two days ago of Tray down at Navy Pier. Her hair was whipping like a gelding's mane in the wind, her dark eyes hidden behind sunglasses. Tray was leaning against a pillar next to one of the river ferries, the collar of her nylon windbreaker pulled up over her neck. She was smiling that bold smile that always made her seem so invulnerable, so much in control of everything she touched. Even pictures could lie, Cole thought, or certainly be misinterpreted.

Tray was anything but in control and Cole knew it. As fiercely as Tray wanted independence, she was far from realizing that desire. Financially, she was unstable and owed everybody money. And although that situation seemed temporary due to legal problems, Cole doubted that Tray would ever be financially stable in a new career. She seemed to have lost her heart and desire to succeed at anything else but medicine.

Cole also worried about Tray's emotional state. She wondered if the last ten months had completely obliterated Tray's confidence and longing to move forward with her life. Further complicating everything else, was Cole's own instinct to try to fix everything for Tray — to make everything in Tray's life okay again. But Cole was finally beginning to realize that she couldn't make everything better for Tray, just like she hadn't been able to make everything better for Jan. As well as she thought she knew both these women, they seemed like strangers to her now.

There was a knock on the darkroom's outside door. It nearly startled Cole out of her skin. Quickly, she stepped into the space between the two doors. Making certain the inner door to the darkroom was closed, she opened the outer door to find Jan. Dressed in a maroon shell and black linen jacket, she had obviously stopped by the house in between appointments.

"Uh, you scared me," Cole said, trying to force a smile. "You look great. How are you?"

Jan folded her arms across her chest. "I'm fine, Cole. I need to talk with you. Mind coming upstairs for a few minutes?"

"No, not at all." Cole removed her work apron and hung it over the banister that led to the first floor. She followed Jan up the steps and into the kitchen.

With businesslike movements, Jan sat down at the kitchen table. There was a manila file folder on the table, which she opened to reveal several sheets of paper. "Sit down." Jan nodded to the seat across from her.

Cole sat down. She felt like an employee who had

been summoned by the boss for a reprimand. A bad feeling crept into the pit of her stomach. "What's up?"

Nervously, Jan clenched and unclenched her hands. "I don't know how to tell you this. But in a strange way, I feel partly responsible."

"What are you talking about?"

"I'm talking about making you unhappy. Driving you away. Of putting doubts inside your heart about us."

Cole scratched her head. "Uh, well, that wasn't all your fault."

"Maybe not. We both could have done some things differently, I'm sure." Jan scanned the papers in front of her. "And now you're going to be hurt again."

"Why? What's wrong?"

"Cole, Tray Roberts is not at all who she claims to be."

"Uh, what do you mean?"

Jan's eyes looked red and glassy, as if she hadn't slept in the past few nights. Her hair, usually combed in soft, wavy curls over her shoulders, was unruly and without its normally lustrous sheen. "I told you I thought there was something funny about Tray — and I meant it. Maybe partly out of spite, but more so out of concern for you."

"Yes," Cole agreed. "We've had this conversation before. I remember it well."

"And so I did something about it. I had her investigated."

Cole's eyes widened with disbelief. She felt her temples throbbing. "You did what?"

"Listen to me, Cole. Before you get angry, just listen to me."

"I'm listening. This better be good."

"It's not good. None of it's good." Jan flipped through the sheets of paper. "First of all, Tray — or maybe I should say Tracy — never graduated from the University of Kentucky or the University of Kentucky Medical College. And she never worked at Grady Hospital in Atlanta."

Cole stared at Jan blankly. She didn't know what to say.

"Tray's been disabled since nineteen-ninety-six. She was not disabled as the result of a car accident nine months ago — although she was in a car accident and was injured. That part of the story is true. But the accident was not the cause of her disability. I have her full report right here."

Jan slid the paper toward Cole and Cole grabbed it, scanning it quickly. "I've seen this paper. It's a mistake. That's what Tray told me. The government's got her mixed up with someone else."

"Not according to what I found out." Jan squeezed Cole's hand. "She also has a criminal record that includes shoplifting, fraud, assault and theft."

"A criminal record?"

"Yes. It's all here. You can keep these reports." Jan turned over the file. "I'm sorry, Cole. Honestly I am."

Cole thumbed through the sheets of paper. She felt like someone was squeezing the life out of her, choking off the air she needed to breathe. According to the reports in front of her, Tray was a complete phony, a pathological liar and criminal to boot. She'd been conning people most of her life — and Cole wasn't the first.

"Listen, Cole. There's more. Tray never lived in

Atlanta — at least not recently. Her last known address was right here in Chicago. I've written it down for you. You might want to check it out."

Cole accepted the small slip of paper from Jan. "Uh, thanks."

"I hope you had her sign a legal note for the money she owes you."

"Not for you to worry about."

"A nice way of saying it's none of my business. Okay. But you be careful. I mean, if you're planning to confront her. She's a bit of a nut, from what I was able to find out. But very smart, too. She's been able to con a lot of people."

"So it seems. Yes, I'll be careful." Cole placed the reports back into the file folder and got up from the table. "Gotta go. Thanks for your help."

"Are you okay?"

"Yes, I'm just fine."

Chapter Twelve

Jackson paced the living room floor while Cole lay on the sofa staring at the ceiling. She had told him the entire story — about Tray and the information she had received from Jan the day before. His face still scarred from the beating, Jackson had listened in stony silence, tears welling in his eyes. Then she and Jackson had fired up Jackson's computer. They logged onto the Internet to search for the Web-site address Tray had just given her two days ago: www.dreamdecorumltd.com.

"Here it is, Cole. There is such a Web site. Hey,

maybe Jan was wrong after all. Maybe there is some kind of mistaken identity."

Cole scanned the site and soon realized that it was a site that marketed not silk floral designs, but decorative home furnishings. "Damn. She doesn't have a Web site. That was a lie, too. Everything was a lie. Even her so-called business."

"Good God," Jackson said. "It's hard to believe. She sure had me fooled — that night she showed us her sketches. The suit, the briefcase."

"I can't believe she used my money to print up bogus business cards and brochures. I'll bet she even bought those damned silk floral arrangements, too. All to make me think she was legitimate."

Jackson continued pacing, every once in a while stopping at the front door to gaze outside. It had been raining heavily for hours, a rain punctuated by severe thunder and lightning.

"What are you going to do, Cole?" he finally asked, still looking out the front door, hands in his back pockets.

Before Cole could answer, she felt her beeper vibrate. She unclipped it from her belt and squinted at the number. It was Tray. She ignored it. Tray had no idea where she was or what she knew.

"Cole, what are you going to do?"

"Jan gave me the address of the woman Tray used to live with before she moved in with her aunt. I'm going to see if I can talk with her. Then, when I'm a little more clear on the facts, I'm going to talk to Tray."

"Do you think Jan's information is accurate?"

"Yes, I do. Quite honestly, I've had some nagging doubts myself lately. I wanted to believe in Tray.

Wanted to help her. Thought she'd had some pretty tough breaks recently. Gosh, I've felt so guilty."

"Why?"

"Because every time these doubts about her would surface, and I'd start asking questions, she'd say something to make me feel like pond scum. Like how much she missed being a doctor. What a hard time she was having starting this new business. How angry she was about her aunt being murdered. It's almost like she knew I was starting to have doubts. Like she could read my thoughts."

"She made you feel sorry for her so you'd keep on helping her."

"Exactly. Like some kind of psychological torture. God, she's good. Such a con-artist."

Jackson walked over to the sofa and sat down on the floor facing her. "It's really shitty what she's done to you, Cole. I don't know any other way to say it."

Cole put her hands behind her head. She continued to stare at the ceiling, not wanting to look at Jackson. If she looked at him, she knew she'd cry. "What hurts most is that she knew I was vulnerable. Lonely. The whole thing with Jan, how low I felt about myself. I was a great target, wasn't I?"

"I'm sure she sensed all of those things and made them work to her advantage."

"Yeah. She did a damned good job of stroking my wounded pride." Cole laughed bitterly and shook her head. "Even if her words were lies, I needed to hear them, needed to feel good about myself again. Pretty pitiful, huh?" Cole finally found the courage to look at Jackson. She barely managed to hold herself together. "Not to mention costly."

"If she wasn't a woman I'd hit her."

"Heck, it wouldn't be worth the effort. You know, I've been thinking. As pitiful as my needs were, Tray's were even more pathetic. It's pretty sad when you have to invent an entire life for yourself because you're so ashamed of the life you've lived." Cole's pager vibrated again. She slid the switch into the off position. "What's she ever going to be, Jackson, except someone who goes from friend to lover to family member, using everyone to get what she can only really give herself? Self-esteem. Pride. Dignity."

"Yeah, but you have to work for those things. Not sponge off others and take advantage of people who care about you."

"Tell that to Tray. She's doing just fine with her own methods, isn't she?"

"For now. Someday, it'll catch up with her."

"Maybe." Cole sat up and ran her fingers through her hair. "Funny thing was, I really cared about her. Still do. Even as angry as I am."

"You're a good person, Cole. Too good for your own good."

"Suddenly, I feel a whole lot better about myself. Maybe I should thank Tray after all. I've got a great job, good friends — and I'm getting better at communicating."

Jackson laughed and kissed her cheek. "That you are. How about something to eat? You must be hungry."

"A little."

"C'mon in the kitchen. I'll make you my famous stir-fry."

"You're going to cook? This is new."

"Okay, I stole the recipe from David. He showed me how to make it. Says I eat too many meals out of boxes."

"Pizza boxes?"

"Something like that."

"Hell, I've had enough new experiences to last me a lifetime. But what's one more between friends?"

"Worst-case scenario, we wash it down with a couple of imported beers."

"Well, what are we waiting for then, chef? Maybe I'll learn something new, too. That appears to be a trend as well."

The next morning Cole called the newspaper from Jackson's house and arranged to have the day off. She showered and dressed, hopped into her car and drove to the corner of Division and Clark Streets. Walking one short block, Cole took the orange line to Jarvis, deciding it was too far to drive during weekday traffic. After consulting a street map, she found that the address Jan had given her was about three blocks from the Jarvis metro stop. After a briskly paced walk, she had no trouble finding the address.

It was a street lined with old row homes made of brick and wood. The sidewalks had just been replaced and new trees had been planted every half block. She hesitated only briefly at the foot of the steps before taking them two at a time to the porch. She rang the bell and waited, noting the cheap plastic porch furniture. Children's toys were scattered in the front yard:

a three-wheeled bike, a Barbie house and other dolls, some play dishes and plastic food. She wondered if she had the correct address.

The woman who finally answered the door was young, maybe in her late twenties. She was petite with short, dark hair and dark eyes to match. Dressed in jeans and a pastel blue cotton shirt, she was chewing gum a mile a minute.

"Can I help you?"

"Uh, yes. I work for the *Tribune*. Cole Evans." Cole extended her hand. "Are you Phyllis Cantner?"

"Yeah. So what?"

"Was wondering if I could ask you some questions." Cole flashed her press badge. "If you don't mind, that is."

"What about?"

"Tray Roberts."

The woman smirked. "What'd she do now? Rob a bank or something?"

"No, not exactly."

"Well, c'mon in. I've got time for a little amusement."

The house was small, but extremely clean. It smelled like lemon wax and cinnamon. There was no particular style to the décor, just a mish-mash of old and new.

"Sit down," Phyllis said, nodding toward the sofa. She sat on an overstuffed chair across from Cole. "You can call me Phil. Everyone else does," she explained, cracking her gum.

"Uh, sure. Thanks."

Phil, still chewing her gum, lit one of those really thin cigars. The smells of lemon and cinnamon gave way to the aroma of cherry tobacco. "So, whaddya wanna know about Tray Roberts?"

Cole rested her forearms on her thighs. "Well, I was hoping you could tell me whatever you know. Tray and I have been in a relationship for just a few months. She owes me some money — and I sort of thought I knew her, but don't think I really do." Cole smiled meekly.

"Owes you money?" Phil shook her head and puffed on her cigar. "Lady, Tray owes everybody."

"Really?"

"Listen, we were together for five years. At first Tray worked. We were happy. I got two kids, Shannon and Billy." Phil picked up a photo from the coffee table and handed it to Cole. "They're at their grandmother's right now."

"Nice-looking kids."

"Yeah. They're great." Phil twirled her hair with her forefinger. "Anyways, all of a sudden Tray starts havin' these seizures. Supposedly from an accident she had while workin' some mining job in Kentucky."

"Well, at least that's one thing she told me that was true."

Phil chuckled and waved her hand. "Tray's always had her own version of reality. What was I sayin'?"

"Seizures?"

"Oh, yeah. So, they get these seizures under control with medication. Dilantin, I think it's called. But she applies for disability anyway. Takes her a while, but she finally gets it."

"This dilantin. Does it have any weird side effects?"

"It messed up her sleep habits. Was hard to wake

her up sometimes. Plus, the stuff can ruin your teeth. You really hafta be careful."

"So her teeth didn't get knocked out in the accident?"

"Hell, no. Tray's teeth fell out years ago from the dilantin. Didn't take care of her teeth and let the problems go so long that they were in real bad shape when I gave her the boot."

"What happened after she got the disability?"

"She promised to help watch the kids and at least pay part of the rent with her disability check. Of course, I never saw a dime."

"She wouldn't help pay the rent?"

"No. Bought herself cigarettes, clothes, brand new truck. The one that got demolished in the accident. Ran up my credit cards. Forced me to work two jobs to pay the bills and put food on the table. And I had to ask my own mother for help, which was pretty demoralizin'. Whaddya think of that?"

"Doesn't sound like the relationship was a two-way street."

"It wasn't. Finally I was over it and kicked her out. That's when she moved in with her aunt. Had the accident. Since then, I ain't seen her."

"She never called? Never asked to see the kids?"

"Are you kiddin'? She didn't give a damn about us. There's only one person Tray cares about and that's Tray. Sorry to hafta say it, but it's true."

"You hate to believe that about someone."

"Listen, if you ever get ahold of her disability forms, just read 'em and see what I mean. You'd think she was a cripple and brain dead. She claims she can't work, but she ain't never had any problems goin' to any of the clubs — dancin' and drinkin' until six in the mornin'."

"Now she surfs the Internet all night." Cole sat back and crossed her legs. "So, she was never a doctor."

"Doctor?" Phil laughed until she was holding her sides. "That's what she told you? That she was a doctor?"

"Yes."

"Christ, she never even graduated from college. Once, she got a job as a freakin' medical assistant in some doctor's family practice makin' five bucks an hour. All of a sudden she fancied herself a goddamned doctor. Started givin' everybody and their brother medical advice. But she sure wasn't no doctor. Hell, when we met she was workin' in a burger joint operatin' a French fryer."

"And now I'm in the hole for fifteen thousand dollars."

"Tray owes you fifteen thousand dollars?"

"Yes."

"Good luck getting paid back, sister."

"Claimed she needed it to start a business."

"Business? Oh, brother. That'll be the day."

"Well, I think she was never really serious about it. Just a stall so I'd give her the money. She ended up buying a new car, clothes. Even got her teeth fixed." Cole shook her head. She felt like a fool. "Does she ever tell the truth about anything?"

Phil extinguished the cigar. "Not when she needs money. Or a place to live. Before she met me, she was livin' off some other poor woman. She was about to throw Tray out, too, when I came along."

"She's a pro, then."

"At connin' people?"

"Exactly."

"You bet. She's had a lotta practice at it."

"After her aunt was murdered, I felt so sorry for her. Except for her son, she said she had no family left, no job. Claimed she was trying to start a new life. All I wanted to do was help her."

"I tried to help her, too. By the way, Tray ain't got no son either. That's another fantasy of hers — and I ain't never been able to figure that one out. She's got some real mental problems. Needs to get some help, but she ain't never going to."

Cole felt a headache coming on. Almost every word that had come from Tray Roberts' mouth had been a lie.

"Listen, Tray's greatest weapon is guilt. The 'oh woe is me' syndrome. She uses it real well. Don't feel bad. You seem like a nice person. That's your only fault, if it is one."

"I feel like a damned fool."

"I did, too. Seems like we both really cared about her. Took me a long time to break free of her spell. If it makes you feel any better, you've joined a pretty long list of wronged women."

"I don't think that makes me feel any better. But thanks for all your help anyway."

"No problem. Was nice meetin' you. Sorry we met because of Tray."

"So am I."

* * * * *

For hours Cole drove around the city without a destination in mind. What Jan told her two days earlier and what Phil had told her hours earlier was all still sinking in when she finally parked the car about two blocks from Tray's house. Her emotions had swung wildly between anger and pity, hurt and indifference. Much of the anger was directed at herself. For running away from Jan and from her own feelings. For falling prey to guilt and deception.

Cole found Tray upstairs, working on the computer. Immediately, Tray sensed her presence, abruptly turning her chair around. She removed the cigarette from her mouth and brushed the errant red curls from her forehead.

"Hey, babe. Where the hell have you been for the last two days?" Tray jumped up and grabbed Cole's arm. "Scared the livin' shit outta me. I've been beepin' you every damned hour."

Cole jerked her arm from Tray's grasp. "I know. Been staying over at Jackson's."

"Do you think you could've let me know that? I was thinkin' you were dead in an alley somewhere."

"Sorry."

"That's just great." Tray sat back down. "Meanwhile, in between worryin' about your ass, I've been tryin' to close this deal with the Holiday Inn for a day and a half now." Tray shook her head. "Man, it's sure tough makin' a livin' these days."

"Well, you've been a little out of practice, haven't you, Tray? Years out of practice."

"What're you talkin' about?"

"You can quit all the bullshit now. I know all

about you. The disability claim dating back to nineteen-ninety-six. The fact that you never finished college, never got a medical degree. That you've never practiced medicine in any state — at least not as a licensed physician."

Tray dragged long and hard on her cigarette. "Is that right?" she asked defiantly.

"Yes, that's right. No mistake about it. According to the information I have, you worked in the medical field as a . . ." Cole stopped to consult the papers in her folder ". . . medical assistant. That's what it says here. That would have been right after the job at Burger King. You worked as a medical assistant for about a year before you filed for permanent disability. Epilepsy, right?"

"Listen, what part of 'the government's got my records all screwed up' didn't you understand?" Tray growled. "What you're readin' from are the records of another Tracy Roberts. There are about a billion of us out there."

"But how many of you were born in Kentucky and worked in the coal mines?" Cole smiled sardonically. "Which, by the way, is just about the only part of your story that's actually true."

Tray's voice rose in pitch and volume. "Where do you get off havin' the 'tude from hell with me? I don't have to listen to this shit."

"I'm afraid you do," Cole said calmly. "If I have an attitude problem, it's because it's justified."

"Listen, you're supposed to be my girlfriend and my friend. If you don't believe me and have faith in me — that's a pretty sad statement about our relationship."

"Our relationship is over."

"Oh, really? And who filled your head with all this shit in the first place?" Gesturing wildly, Tray jerked herself out of the chair. Her eyes blended from brown to black. "Jan? Is she the one that's got you believin' all this crap? She wouldn't have any ulterior motives, now would she?"

"No, Jan has no ulterior motives, except that she loves me and wants to protect me. I don't think Phil Cantner has any ulterior motives either." The mention of the name made Tray stiffen in her tracks. "You're the one who's filled my head with all the shit and lies. Made me feel sorry for you so I'd lend you money under false pretenses. Well, you've got the loan papers and I expect you to sign them — and pay me back every dime you owe me according to the terms we set from the very beginning."

Tray stared at the loan papers, which were lying on the desk next to the computer. Slowly, she looked back at Cole. "You know, for once I thought I'd met someone special. Someone different. But you're no different than any of the others."

"Different? Different in what way? That I'd let you walk all over me indefinitely? Use me to your heart's content?"

"Someone who'd believe in me and give me a chance, instead of judgin' me."

"You make that very difficult to do, Tray. Did it ever occur to you to tell the truth for once?"

Tray looked her up and down like she was human trash. "No, I was wrong about you. You're no different than any of the others. In fact, you're worse."

"You can quit with the guilt trip. I've had my fill of it. Poor, poor Tray. What a miserable life you've led."

"Fuck you, Cole."

"You've already done that, Tray, in more ways than one."

Grabbing the loan papers, Tray ripped them up. "See if you ever get one dime back from me, bitch! I don't owe you a damned thing."

Cole felt her face flush with anger, but she remained calm. "Play it whichever way you like."

"Sure, it's okay that I cleaned the house, cooked for you, ran your errands. You didn't even have to pay rent."

"Have you lost your mind? You did things for me only when you felt like it, Tray. You act as though you were my personal slave."

"Wasn't I?"

"Since when does anybody run Tray Roberts' life? And, in case you've forgotten, I've been paying the bills here for months now."

"Didn't know you were gonna squeeze me for every fuckin' dime."

"Squeeze you?" Cole closed her eyes and prayed for the strength to walk away. To just walk away. "You know, I really cared about you. That's the sad part. Cared enough to help you, encourage you and worry about you. Enough to put myself in financial jeopardy. I thought you'd been dealt some pretty tough blows — and I worried myself sick over you."

"Well, we'll have a goddamned medal commissioned for you, Cole. I'll pin it on you myself."

"You just keep replaying the same scenes again and again, don't you? I really feel sorry for the next poor slob."

Tray's eyes darkened and her voice became shrill. "Get the hell out. And keep the hell away from me."

"Oh, we're not finished yet, Tray. Maybe for the moment. But we'll see each other again. You can count on it."

Chapter Thirteen

Cole felt like a stranger in her own house. She opened the door cautiously and stepped into the foyer. The lights were off in the living room, but she saw the flickering of the television screen and could barely hear the sound of voices coming from the set.

She dropped her sports bag full of clothing just inside the front door and quietly entered the living room. Jan was asleep on the sofa. For a few moments, Cole thought about running away — of going back to Jackson's to stay for a while. But that would just delay the inevitable.

After visiting and confronting Tray earlier that evening, she had driven to the paper and worked in the darkroom for almost two hours. Marty was puzzled to see her.

"Cole, what're you doing here? Thought you took the day off." He sneezed into a large, white handkerchief. His short, barrel-like body waddled toward her. "You upset or something?"

"No. Just thought I'd use the paper's darkroom for a project I need to get finished. A special series Sheila and Barnes asked me to do."

"Ahhh, I see." Marty rubbed his painfully sore looking nose with the back of his hand. "But you're sure there's nothing I can do for you? You seem . . . well, not quite like your old self."

"I'm fine, Marty. Nothing a little hard work and solitude won't cure."

"Okay, I hear you. Get lost, right?"

Cole slipped into a leather apron. "Tie my apron for me — and then get lost, okay?"

Marty's chest heaved with raspy laughter. "No problem. But you let me know if there's anything old Marty can do for you. Anything at all."

"Thanks, Marty. I appreciate it."

What she'd decided while working in the darkroom had not been earth-shattering or surprising. She wanted to come back home and live with Jan. Unsure of what that meant, Cole was willing to find out — even if it meant sleeping on the futon in the den. She had suddenly realized that facing the truth, even if it was painful, was better than dealing with lies and deception. The truth sometimes hurt, but at least it was real.

Sitting down on the floor next to the sofa, she

watched Jan sleep. She looked tranquil, fragile, beautiful. Cole reached out and gently rubbed Jan's arm. In a few moments, Jan's eyes opened and she smiled.

"Cole, what are you doing here? It's late, isn't it?"

"Late. But not too late."

"Did you forget something?"

"Yes, in a way."

"What?"

"How much I've missed you. Exactly how much you mean to me."

Jan's eyes glistened. "I've missed you too, Cole. But maybe your leaving me was the best thing. It kind of brought me to my senses."

Cole wrapped her arms around her knees and nodded. "I understand."

"It made me wonder what I'd been searching for, when all the time it was right here with me." A single tear fell and rolled down Jan's cheek. "I think it's sad when you have to lose someone to make you realize what an idiot you've been."

"I don't think trying to get to know yourself better qualifies you as an idiot. I'm the one who's been an idiot. I should have been more supportive, more understanding."

"You were hurt."

"And did my share of hurting, too. So, what do I do? Blunder forward without looking both ways. Guess I got what I deserved."

Jan sat up and rubbed her eyes. She leaned her face in her hands, resting her elbows on her thighs. "Cole, I admit to being confused about us and not always knowing why. When I was younger, my home life wasn't very pleasant. I know you understand that because you've been gracious enough to listen over the years and be comforting where that's concerned."

"You don't owe me an explanation."

"Maybe not. But I think you have a right to know about the turmoil that's been churning inside of me ever since I was a kid. I've given you a pretty hard time about your lack of communication with me. And now here I sit — the one with everything to say, realizing that I've done a pretty poor job myself."

"It doesn't always take a lot of words."

"No, it doesn't. But I'm used to having everything screamed at me. That's how my family communicated. By screaming, yelling, badgering. By making life a continuous battleground. You'd think I'd appreciate silence."

"Silence to you isn't normal."

"I mistake it for apathy." Jan smiled and folded the throw blanket. "For all the screaming and yelling my family did, we still loved one another. Maybe we were dysfunctional to some degree, but we still cared."

"I care about you, too."

Jan looked up and her eyes flashed vibrantly blue in the glint of the television screen. "Are you going to come home?"

"I'd like to."

"It's where you belong."

"I know."

Jan held out her hand and Cole grasped it. The touch was lovingly familiar.

Three weeks later, Cole stopped into Temptations, a lesbian club located near Franklin Park. She had arranged to meet Kay and some of her friends for a drink.

"Hey, babe!" Kay said as Cole rounded the corner to the bar on the other side of the room. "Good to see you!" Kay kissed Cole on the cheek and introduced her to three of her friends, Deb, Tammy and Rita.

"Nice to meet you," Cole smiled, shaking their hands. "Thanks for inviting me."

"Kay's told us so much about you," Rita said, fluttering her long, brown eyelashes. Her blond hair was a short, Meg Ryan cut. "I see she didn't tell any lies."

"Uh, well, I hope Kay didn't give me too big of a buildup. I'd have to quit sharing disaster photos with her."

Kay laughed and slapped Cole on the back. She handed Cole a beer and said to her group of friends, "Watch it. This one's crazy. She's going to break her pretty neck one of these days, jumping around rooftops."

"Not with you there to catch me, Kay."

The women laughed and teased Kay. Cole wrapped a napkin around the cold beer bottle. Out of the corner of her eye, she caught a glimpse of the dance floor to her left. There were several small tables set up along its edge. It was the wild, red hair that first caught her attention. Then the gestures and hoarse laughter. Across the room, Tray Roberts sat at a table with a much younger woman, talking a mile a minute, laughing, smoking and generally being true to form. Cole was transfixed. The sight was eerie. Even though it had taken place at a different location, Cole felt a powerful sensation of déjà vu. She imagined herself sitting there not more than ten months earlier, listening to the same stories, drawn and beguiled into that carefully strung web of lies and deceit. Months ago the lies had been hidden by charm, covered up with guilt and disguised by friendship, and later by love.

The young woman who listened to Tray appeared attentive and wide-eyed, hanging on every word. She was already smitten, Cole thought. But maybe it wasn't too late to inflict just a little damage to the foundation of trust that had already been laid.

Rita had sidled up next to her. "Got your eye on someone," she asked in a disappointed tone.

"Yes. Can you hang onto this for me?" Cole handed Rita her beer. "I'll be right back."

"Promise?" Rita asked, feigning a pout.

"Promise."

Cole approached the table with an easy stride. After all, what more could Tray possibly do to her? All the lies had been told, the money spent, the hurt dished out.

"Dr. Roberts, how nice to see you this evening," Cole said with a distinct edge of sarcasm.

The cigarette in Tray's mouth hit the table, ashes scattering. Then it rolled onto the floor. Tray bent over and picked it up, throwing it into an ashtray. "Miss Evans, how are you?" she asked through the teeth Cole had paid for.

"Just fine. Aren't you going to introduce me to your friend?"

"Yeah, sure. This is Jennifer."

Cole smiled broadly. "My pleasure."

"Hi. Nice to meet you," Jennifer replied.

"Tray, I just wanted to inquire about the fifteen thousand dollars you owe me. You remember. The money that paid for your false teeth, car, living expenses and God knows what else. Haven't heard from you and I need to be paid back soon."

Jennifer looked confused. "False teeth? Money? Ummm, what's she talkin about, Tray?" She was young — in her mid-twenties at the most. Her eyelids fluttered nonstop. Cole couldn't stop staring at the purple lipstick.

Tray looked at Jennifer, then at Cole. "This ain't the time nor place to discuss business," she growled.

Cole leaned her hand on the table. "Why? Too busy telling your 'I used to be a doctor' stories?"

"Tray did used to be a doctor," Jennifer said proudly. "Real important one in Atlanta."

Cole smirked. "Well, at least your lies are consistent, Tray."

"Lies?" Jennifer frowned.

"Tray may have been a doctor," Cole said coldly, "in a former life, but not in this lifetime."

Jennifer looked at Tray, then back at Cole.

"It's okay, babe," Tray said to Jennifer with a reassuring glance. "Cole got her ass dumped by me, so she's kinda bitter."

Cole shook her head in disbelief. "You're a piece of work, Tray. But you're the one who has to live with yourself. You can use lovers and betray your friends and lie to everyone, including yourself. In the final analysis, it doesn't change who you are."

Tray got up and grabbed Jennifer by the arm. "C'mon, we're leavin'."

"Oh, please. Don't leave on my account," Cole said, backing away from the table. She turned and started to walk away and then swung around again. "By the way. It was worth losing fifteen thousand dollars to be rid of you, Tray — and to find out who the most important person in my life really is. Good night."

Kay was waiting for Cole when she got back to the bar. "Hey, what was all that about?"

"That's Tray. Remember, we talked about her when we had coffee last week."

"Oh, yeah. I remember. Now I know why the name's familiar, 'cause the face is, too."

"You know her?"

"Let's put it this way, I know of her. She used to date the friend of a friend. That is, until she borrowed some money and never paid it back."

"Damn her. She really gets around, doesn't she?"

"Yep. Seems like she's trying to get around some more."

"Unfortunately. And it's really no use trying to warn the poor woman, other than what I just did. I'm afraid she'll have to find out on her own what kind of person Tray Roberts really is."

"She will."

"I have no doubt about that." Cole turned to locate her beer.

"Here, Cole," Rita said, handing it to her. She ran her finger up and down Cole's arm. "Wanna dance?"

Kay put her hand on Rita's shoulder. "Listen, you're gonna have to behave yourself, kid. I have a funny feeling Cole's taken again." Kay looked over at Cole and smiled. "Am I right, my friend?"

"Yes, you are. You definitely are."

Cole glanced at the digital clock in her car. It was ten of eleven. The accident just ahead had slowed down traffic for a couple of miles along Lake Shore Drive. To make matters worse, several cars had overheated. It was a sticky, humid July night and people's tempers were at breaking point. For more than forty-five minutes, Cole had crawled along in disbelief that she was going to be late for her first official day on the job as a *Trib* employee. Even after reconciling with Jan and being faced with no more living expenses than she had before, she felt strongly that the time was right to give up her freelance status and join the staff officially. Besides, she had a fifteen-thousand-dollar loan to pay back over the next five years.

Now, for the first time she was going to be late for a deadline. The irony made her laugh out loud. Suddenly, the traffic began to move as cars were detoured off the next exit.

When she finally arrived downtown, Cole pulled into the parking garage and hurried to catch the elevator. As the doors slid open to the fifth floor, she rushed from the hallway, through the double doors and back to the photo lab. The place seemed eerily quiet. A few people were at their desks, talking on the phone or peering at their computer screens.

The photo lab doors opened into a sea of people. There were streamers hung across the ceiling, a table covered with food, refreshments and cake.

"Surprise!" everyone yelled. Cole stopped and surveyed the room. Jan was there. Jackson and David. Even Kay from the *Sun-Times*. Sheila, Barnes, Marty, Donna. A sizable contingent of the city news staff, including writers, reporters, columnists and administrative personnel were jammed into the large space.

There were no strangers here, Cole thought. Not anymore.

Sheila stepped out of the crowd and reached for the envelope Cole held at her side. "You're late, Miss Evans. It's not nice to keep your coworkers waiting."

"Uh, gosh. I'm sorry." Cole looked at the floor and shrugged. "You see, there was this accident on Lake Shore Drive —"

"Welcome to the team, Cole," Sheila interrupted. "Better late than never." Smiling, Sheila shook Cole's hand. "We're very pleased to have you with us officially. We hope you'll be with us for many years to come."

"Uh, thanks. I'm honored. Really."

"No sense asking for a speech," Kay bellowed. "You'll never get one outta Cole. Might as well eat."

Cole laughed along with everyone else. She gratefully accepted hugs and congratulations from her friends and colleagues. Then Jan helped her cut the huge sheet cake decorated with the *Tribune's* red, white and blue banner.

Sliding the first piece of cake onto a small paper plate, Jan handed it to Cole. "Welcome home, Cole. In more ways than one."

"Thanks," Cole answered. "I feel like I've just walked back into my life. And it feels great."

LOOKING FOR NAIAD?

A few of the publications of
THE NAIAD PRESS, INC.
P.O. Box 10543   Tallahassee, Florida 32302
Phone (850) 539-5965
Toll-Free Order Number: 1-800-533-1973
Web Site: WWW.NAIADPRESS.COM
Mail orders welcome. Please include 15% postage.
Write or call for our free catalog which also features an
incredible selection of lesbian videos.

INTIMATE STRANGER by Laura DeHart Young. 192 pp.
Ignoring Tray's myserious past, could Cole be playing with fire?
ISBN 1-56280-249-6 $11.95

SHATTERED ILLUSIONS by Kaye Davis. 256 pp. 4th
Maris Middleton mystery.   ISBN 1-56280-252-6   11.95

SETUP by Claire McNab. 240 pp. 11th Detective Inspector Carol
Ashton mystery.   ISBN 1-56280-255-0   11.95

THE DAWNING by Laura Adams. 224 pp. What if you had the
power to change the past?   ISBN 1-56280-246-1   11.95

NEVER ENDING by Marianne Martin. 224 pp. Temptation
appears in the form of an old friend and lover. ISBN 1-56280-247-X   11.95

ONE OF OUR OWN by Diane Salvatore. 240 pp. Carly Matson
has a secret. So does Lela Johns.   ISBN 1-56280-243-7   11.95

DOUBLE TAKEOUT by Tracey Richardson. 176 pp. 3rd Stevie
Houston mystery.   ISBN 1-56280-244-5   11.95

CAPTIVE HEART by Frankie J. Jones. 176 pp. Love in the
fast lane or heartside romance?   ISBN 1-56280-258-5   11.95

WICKED GOOD TIME by Diana Tremain Braund. 224 pp. In
charge at work, out of control in her heart.   ISBN 1-56280-241-0   11.95

SNAKE EYES by Pat Welch. 256 pp. 7th Helen Black mystery.
ISBN 1-56280-242-9   11.95

CHANGE OF HEART by Linda Hill. 176 pp. High fashion and
love in a glamorous world.   ISBN 1-56280-238-0   11.95

UNSTRUNG HEART by Robbi Sommers. 176 pp. Putting life
in order again.   ISBN 1-56280-239-9   11.95

BIRDS OF A FEATHER by Jackie Calhoun. 240 pp. Life begins
with love.   ISBN 1-56280-240-2   11.95

THE DRIVE by Trisha Todd. 176 pp. The star of *Claire of the
Moon* tells all!   ISBN 1-56280-237-2   11.95

BOTH SIDES by Saxon Bennett. 240 pp. A community of
women falling in and out of love.   ISBN 1-56280-236-4   11.95

WATERMARK by Karin Kallmaker. 256 pp. One burning
question . . . how to lead her back to love?   ISBN 1-56280-235-6   11.95

THE OTHER WOMAN by Ann O'Leary. 240 pp. Her roguish
way draws women like a magnet.   ISBN 1-56280-234-8   11.95

SILVER THREADS by Lyn Denison.208 pp. Finding her way
back to love . . .   ISBN 1-56280-231-3   11.95

CHIMNEY ROCK BLUES by Janet McClellan. 224 pp. 4th Tru
North mystery.   ISBN 1-56280-233-X   11.95

OMAHA'S BELL by Penny Hayes. 208 pp. Orphaned Keeley
Delaney woos the lovely Prudence Morris.   ISBN 1-56280-232-1   11.95

SIXTH SENSE by Kate Calloway. 224 pp. 6th Cassidy James
mystery.   ISBN 1-56280-228-3   11.95

DAWN OF THE DANCE by Marianne K. Martin. 224 pp. A dance
with an old friend, nothing more . . . yeah!   ISBN 1-56280-229-1   11.95

WEDDING BELL BLUES by Julia Watts. 240 pp. Love, family,
and a recipe for success.   ISBN 1-56280-230-5   11.95

THOSE WHO WAIT by Peggy J. Herring. 160 pp. Two
sisters . . . in love with the same woman.   ISBN 1-56280-223-2   11.95

WHISPERS IN THE WIND by Frankie J. Jones. 192 pp. "If you
don't want this," she whispered, "all you have to say is 'stop.' "
                                                 ISBN 1-56280-226-7   11.95

WHEN SOME BODY DISAPPEARS by Therese Szymanski.
192 pp. 3rd Brett Higgins mystery.   ISBN 1-56280-227-5   11.95

THE WAY LIFE SHOULD BE by Diana Braund. 240 pp. Which
one will teach her the true meaning of love?   ISBN 1-56280-221-6   11.95

UNTIL THE END by Kaye Davis. 256pp. 3rd Maris Middleton
mystery.   ISBN 1-56280-222-4   11.95

FIFTH WHEEL by Kate Calloway. 224 pp. 5th Cassidy James
mystery.   ISBN 1-56280-218-6   11.95

JUST YESTERDAY by Linda Hill. 176 pp. Reliving all the
passion of yesterday.   ISBN 1-56280-219-4   11.95

THE TOUCH OF YOUR HAND edited by Barbara Grier and
Christine Cassidy. 304 pp. Erotic love stories by Naiad Press
authors.   ISBN 1-56280-220-8   14.95

These are just a few of the many Naiad Press titles — we are the oldest and
largest lesbian/feminist publishing company in the world. We also offer an
enormous selection of lesbian video products. Please request a complete
catalog. We offer personal service; we encourage and welcome direct mail
orders from individuals who have limited access to bookstores carrying our
publications.